MW01221758

MORE FROM
THE CHAMPAGNE WRITERS OF SHROPSHIRE

Stories and Poems

by

Rosemarie David

Liz Penn

Louise McClean

Maureen Thomas

Carol Campbell

Sue Whiting

Ruth Broster

Phyl Furniss

Olga Tramontin

Edited by Geoffrey Thatcher

ISBN 978-0-9929577-2-8

Published by Chadgreen Publishing Limited, Telford

Printed and bound in Great Britain by
Think Ink Limited, Ipswich, Suffolk

Contents

Jubani – an African child
by Rosemarie David

It was cold and he shivered. He was afraid. Why were they taking so long to come back? The cave was dark and lonely. He looked down at his skinny arms covered in goose bumps. There was a splash as a tear landed on his dusty dark skin. Perhaps a lion had eaten them or they had got lost in the dark. A movement from the entrance of the cave startled him and he backed against the hard stone wall. There was a grunt followed by a big furry body that leapt at him. A long wet tongue slurped along his cheek and the child threw his arms around the huge neck in relief. It was Shamwari[1], the family dog. He felt safer now but where were his family? His Father had gone to hunt for food two days ago and his Mother went to collect water from the river the day before but she had not returned. Shamwari lay down and the child curled up beside him snuggling into his warmth. They slept.

In the morning a ray of sun shone through the entrance of the cave waking the child. He stood up stretching and yawning. Shamwari ~~Rosemarie~~ rose too, shook himself and went outside followed by the little boy. The dog's feet padded along the dry path as he walked towards the nearby river to drink. The rocky outcrops were silent and the tall yellow grass stood still. The child followed the shaggy animal to the river and drank too. Then he went in search of something to eat. A few wild berries were all he could find and he went back to the cave and sat outside in the sunshine. Shamwari returned with a bird in his jaws and ripped it open at the boy's feet. The child reached down and pulled a chunk of warm flesh from the carcass. As he stuffed it hungrily into his mouth the fresh blood ran down his chin but he ignored it as he reached for another piece.

---

[1] Shamwari – Friend

The day passed slowly and Jubani cried for his family but Shamwari stayed close and he did not feel afraid. Another night passed and in the morning the dog was gone. The child was alone again. He rubbed his tear stained face and then he started to walk away from the cave. He needed help and instinct led him as he walked through the dense bush. There was no sign of his Mother or his Father. He knew that the dog would find him when he went back to the cave later that day as he would follow the child's scent. Sweat ran down the boy's body leaving streaks in the dust and his mouth was dry but he walked on. He reasoned that his Mother must have been taken by the crocodile at the river and that he would not see her again. That is what had happened to his Gogo[2] a few months ago and when he cried his Mother had told him that all creatures needed to eat and he must be very careful at rivers. His Father would have been home by now unless he was hurt and unable to come back, so Jubani was alone, except for the dog who would return when he had finished hunting.

As the day drew to a close a dark cloak enveloped the savannah and the boy knew he must find a place to sleep. He had left the rocky outcrops and caves far behind him but there were many thorn trees around and he climbed into one of these and shrugged himself into a safe cradle of branches. The night was alive with noises. Jackal's yelped and lions grunted. There were the screams of small furry creatures as owls swooped down and sank their talons into them. Shamwari found him just before dawn and the child jumped down from the tree and hugged him with relief. As they walked along together the child began to stumble. He was growing weaker, he could not continue for much longer. Later that day as he sat down to rest in the shade of a thorn tree he knew that he would not get up again. Shamwari tried to rouse him

---

[2] Gogo – Granny

but in vain. Jubani had decided that it was time to die and that was what he would do.

His Mother had indeed been killed by the crocodile and his Father had been attacked by a lion but although his injuries were severe some local natives had cared for him and after searching he found his son and the dog Shamwari later that day. The boy was close to death when he was lifted by a strong pair of hands and carried close to a solid warm chest. "Baba"[3] the child whispered and touching the beloved face with his tiny fingers he began to cry. His Father hugged him and the dear familiar face leant forward to touch his. Shamwari gambolled about them both as they made their way home.

Tapped Up
by Liz Penn

Bill could not believe he was standing in such an elegant home, everything about it spelled money. He was here because the person on the phone had sounded so desperate with the report of water coming through the kitchen ceiling.

After locating the address in his 'A to Z' Bill had come right away, he realised he was needed urgently.

He had come to the right house, but couldn't hear anything untoward, no clanging of pipes, no splashing of water, just absolute silence, he felt uneasy and didn't like the quiet.

Then he saw her. What she was wearing was flimsy and he could see the outline of a very shapely figure. 'My husband let you in, please follow me.'

So he did follow her. Up the very grand stairway, along the landing, and into a picture-book bathroom. She came up close to him, brushing

---

[3] Baba – Father

9

his shoulder with her arm, then asked him to examine the bath taps, as the ceiling below was getting drips and could he see to mending them. All the time, she was fluttering her eye lashes and gently touching him, almost flirting outrageously. Bill felt most uncomfortable and told her that he had his toolbox in the van with his kit of spare washers; he would go and get them and try to effect a satisfactory repair.

He sat in the comfort of his little red van, deciding whether to go back into the house or start up the engine and go home. However, his conscience got the better of him and with a big sigh he strode back up to the house.

This time the door was open, Bill heard voices and then 'HE' appeared on the stairs. 'Go away!' HE shouted, and Bill started to explain that he'd come to fix the taps and stop them from leaking. 'We don't need you,' was the harsh reply.

Bill turned to walk away and with the light shining in through the door, he noticed for the first time the bright red stain on the man's shirt; he guessed what it was.

Back in his van Bill revved up and sped away. His thoughts were racing. Was he heading home or to the nearest Police Station? He knew he would have to decide… as soon as he could think straight.

The New Neighbours
by Louise McClean

Mabel found the thought of new neighbours very disconcerting. Your neighbours were so important: they had the power to make your life liveable or miserable. Mabel and Harry's old ones, Mr and Mrs Green, had lived there for over twenty years. Like them, they had no children and they were very quiet and no trouble at all. They had spoken to each other over the garden fence in the summer, but had never entered each other's houses of course – that would be an invasion of privacy in Mabel's eyes. But Mrs Green had suddenly passed away and Mr Green had gone to live with his sister up north somewhere.

The FOR SALE sign had been up for a couple of months and Mabel had anxiously watched the various people who had been to view the house. This had involved being in the front garden a lot, pretending you were busily weeding and not really looking or listening to what was going on.

Some of them had been very odd indeed, like the two men who had held hands as they came up the path. Mabel sniffed, she knew what that meant thank you, and Harry and she wanted nothing like that next door – it wasn't natural.

Then there had been the bleached blonde with the short skirt and the two children but no sign of a husband. Mabel knew what that meant too and she certainly didn't approve of single mothers – they were nothing but trouble.

But the most worrying of all was the Indian family. They looked clean enough, but Mabel just knew there would be dozens of them and the smell of curry would come through the walls. She and Harry didn't care for foreign food. It was all very disturbing for Mabel, though strangely Harry seemed to be taking it all in his stride – typical male, thought Mabel, and sniffed.

Thankfully, none of these potential buyers had returned, but the man in the paper shop told Harry the house had been sold to a family called James, but that was all she knew about them, except that they had two children, which in itself was worrying.

Mabel anxiously awaited their arrival and on moving day she was behind her net curtains, watching their every move. She didn't approve of women wearing jeans, but the couple looked tidy enough and their car was clean, which was a good sign. There didn't seem to be a lot of furniture and it was all modern – no real quality there, thought Mabel, sniffing. There was no sign of the two children yet.

Later in the afternoon, Mabel thought of sending in a tray of tea, but then decided not to. Maybe this young woman would take advantage of Mabel's good nature and think she could start to run in and out of Mabel's house all the time. It was better to nip anything like that in the bud before it became a problem, she decided.

The days and months ahead would be like a minefield, so many things could go wrong. The children could be noisy or cheeky and kick balls into Mabel's garden. Maybe they would play music loudly, or have the TV on late at night; you could never tell. They might not keep the garden tidy and then the weeds would spread to Mabel's garden. Goodness, for all Mabel knew, they might not even be married because Mabel knew that sort of thing went on all the time now, and she certainly wouldn't want to get too close to anybody like that.

No, thought Mabel, she would bide her time for a couple of months and see how things went. In the meantime, she would just nod to them if they were out in the garden at the same time, and she would make sure Harry did the same. After all, you knew nothing about new neighbours, and you couldn't be too careful, could you?

Mabel folded her arms, sniffed, and drew back from the window.

A Dark Night
by Maureen Thomas

It was a very dark and windy night with no moonlight to guide them. Tommy and his two friends, George and Harry, had sneaked out of their houses to meet here at the entrance to the woods. Tommy had brought along his father's torch, his friends had forgotten to do the same. 'Typical,' Tommy thought. They explained that they were so excited at the thought of going to the so called 'haunted' woods, that it had completely slipped their minds. 'Never mind,' he said. 'We're all here and no one has chickened out.' They had heard about these woods and the fact that there was something horrible was lurking in and around them. That fact didn't scare them... or so they thought. As they stood at the edge of the woods, Tommy shone his father's torch upwards to the very top of the trees and they all saw that the wind was shaking the branches. They looked like giant bony fingers and they seemed to be beckoning the boys into their domain, and the leaves that fell onto their faces as they looked upwards felt like crispy kisses. They shuddered.

Tommy was a little bit scared of the dark but he would not show this fact to his friends, he was just so glad that they were there to keep him company. They all stared in front of them into the darkness of the woods. What was that noise? Was it the rustle of the leaves? Or was it the THING that stood behind them watching from a distance? When Tommy shone his torch all around them, they saw the THING lumbering towards them. It was HUGE! Tommy and his two friends were huddling together and screaming... AAAARGH!

They all ran into the woods and made it into a thick bush where they hid in the hope that the THING would go away. They were shivering now and their teeth were chattering. Goose bumps formed all over their bodies and, worst of all, Tommy had dropped his father's torch!

The THING was getting closer, they could hear it panting as it lumbered towards them. They sat as quietly as they could. But that didn't work. It must have been able to smell their fear. Oh, how they all wished they were tucked up in their nice warm beds right now.

The THING stopped right by the bush where they were all huddled together: it was panting, and they could almost touch it if they wanted... but they did NOT! Then something strange happened, the THING let out a monster roar and the branches of the bush where they were hiding opened up and two hideous eyes were looking down on them and the THING said 'Thank goodness I've found you. I saw you go out of the house and decided to follow you. You were very quick so I had to run to keep up.'

The IT was Tommy's father and, boy, were they all glad to see him. 'Come on you lot, you're safe now, let's get you home.'

Tommy and his friends timidly came out of the bush and they went home to a cup of hot chocolate and a lovely warm bed. Tommy had learned his lesson, and for sneaking out of the house without permission? His father dealt with him the next morning. As for the THING, it is still there.

New Beginnings
by Carol Campbell

Each day is a new beginning
We have left yesterday
And now today has arrived
We can't now live tomorrow today
And can't live yesterday today as that won't change
The only changing we can do is in the present
Not the past.
So make the most of what you have
And enjoy living in the present
Not the past which you are unable to change.
Enjoy the light each day brings
And change what you can
But accept there are some things you can't change
Because maybe not everything can or should be changed.

Eyes Wide Shut
by Sue Whiting

'Mummy please tell me the story about your eyes again, pleeeease,' said my daughter Fiona. She was five years old and asked me for this story at least once a month.

'Oh, do I have to darling, you've heard it so many times before?' I was wondering if Horrid Henry would suffice.

'Oh please Mummy, it's my favourite.'

'Ok if you really want me to. Now snuggle down in your bed and cuddle teddy.' I settled myself on the edge of the bed.

'Well the day I was born was a bit of a shock for Nana and Granddad. I had only been in Nana's tummy for six months instead of nine and things started to happen. Nana was a little bit frightened as she knew I was coming too early.'

'How did she know you were coming Mummy?' Fiona asked, very curious.

'Well she had these funny feelings in her tummy, so Granddad took her to the hospital. Then the doctors told her that I was about to be born. Granddad was with Nana, holding her hand, when I came very quickly into the world.

'Did you cry Mummy?'

'Yes I did. Your Granddad told me I made a racket. But there was something wrong; the nurses were huddled around me talking. Nana was worried and she said to your Granddad, 'There's something wrong with the baby I can tell.' The nurses brought me to Nana wrapped in a pink blanket and said, 'Mrs Whiting, as your baby has come so early, she has to go to the premature baby unit.' Nana only had a chance to have a little peek at me, and the first thing she noticed was my beautiful black hair. Nana and Granddad thought I was perfect. But my eyes, they couldn't see my eyes as they were tight shut.

Next morning the doctor came to see Nana on the ward to talk to her. 'Mrs Whiting, your baby is doing very well considering, but it's her eyes...' Nana was so worried what he was going to say next. 'The baby's eyes are sealed shut. We think it is because she came so early. I'm afraid she will never see. I'm sorry.'

Nana was so shocked and upset. A blind baby, she thought, how cruel was that. Granddad arrived and so Nana told him. They were both very upset. Later that morning they came to the premature baby unit to see me. They stared at this beautiful baby who was perfect in every way except one: she couldn't open her eyes. Nana and Granddad cried and cuddled each other for comfort.

As days turned into weeks, then months and years, Nana and Granddad treasured me, even though I could not see. I didn't know any different because, after all, I had never been able to see. They used to describe everything to me and I learned a lot because of that. Plus I could feel things, touch them. They tried so very hard to teach me about colour, but this I found too difficult to understand. Then one day, one very exciting day after I had had lots of tests done at the hospital, the doctor called Nana and Granddad into his office.

'Mr and Mrs Whiting, we've now done extensive tests on your daughter, and we're pretty sure if we can open her eyes, we think she will be able to see.'

Nana and Granddad were so thrilled, and a little frightened, when they left the hospital with me. The operation was to take place the following week. By this time, I was four years old and old enough – Nana thought – to explain to me what was going to happen. I was scared about the operation but also curious as to what my eyes would look like.

'Mummy,' I asked. 'What colour are your eyes?'

Nana told me her eyes were blue.

'And what colour are Daddy's eyes?' She told me his were brown. I thought about this long and hard. 'What colour will my eyes be then?' I asked.

'Well we won't know until after the operation, but they could be blue like mine or brown like Daddy's,' Nana explained.

The night before I went into hospital I lay on my bed thinking. If I had brown eyes like Daddy, perhaps Mummy would be upset. But if I had blue eyes like Mummy what would Daddy think? On the morning of the operation I asked Nana, 'Mummy, what colour do you want my eyes to be? Blue like yours or brown like Daddy's?'

Nana thought for a moment, then said to me, 'My darling little girl, as long as your eyes are perfect and you can see, I honestly don't mind what colour they will be. I just know they will be beautiful.'

It was a long, delicate operation and Nana and Granddad sat in the Parents' Room holding hands. Then the doctor who did the operation entered the room. 'Mr and Mrs Whiting,' he said. 'I am pleased to tell you that the procedure has gone very well. We won't know how her sight is until the bandages come off in two days time. But we are very hopeful.'

When I woke up I was a bit sore, but so excited. The two days passed quickly and it was time for them to remove my bandages. Nana held my hand and kept telling me everything would be all right. Then the great moment came. The doctor told me to try and open my eyes. I gradually managed to open them, but immediately felt so confused. I could see, but there was so much to look at.

'Mummy, I can see... but... things are a bit... muddled,' I said, and there was fear in my voice. The doctor told them it would take time for my eyes to adjust, but he was very hopeful.

I looked at Nana and then at Granddad and I could see their eyes: see the brown and the blue. And mine? Were they brown or blue? I was almost too afraid to ask, because I liked both their colours. In hushed tones I whispered to Nana, 'What colour are my eyes, Mummy?'

'Well darling,' she replied, 'you have a very rare thing, something that doesn't happen very often. It's because you're so special you have one blue eye and one brown.'

It made me the happiest girl in the whole wide world. So that's the end of my story, with such a happy ending.'

'Mummy,' my now sleepy daughter whispered. 'That's why we're so special isn't it? Because I've got the same eyes as you.'

'It is indeed darling, now it's time to go to sleep. Night night, sleep tight.'

'Night night Mummy, I love you.'

'I love you too princess.'

A Mother's Pain
by Ruth Broster

It's thoughtless to say I never knew you,
When really I did,
You charmed the socks off me,
Ever since you were a kid.
The dark has clouded over and swept you away,
The distance between us was unexpected in this way.
For who knows the future not you or I,
We may never see each other or see eye to eye.
There is one thing for sure I know in my heart,
That I was your first love although we're apart,
The day you were born the bond we met,
I don't really think we will ever forget.

Miss Tappenden
by Phyl Furniss

Miss Tappenden owned the sweet shop at the end of a small row of shops in Halford Terrace. People that knew her called her Miss Tapp. She was a thin woman, with grey hair that she plaited at each side of her head, then wind them into a circle and pin them over her ears with many hairpins. Her glasses were thin rimmed and perched on the end of her nose. She always wore a clean white apron over her dark dress.

The shop was generously full of sweet jars, some of which were on the high shelves at the back of the counter. She needed a pair of steps to reach these: they contained bulls' eyes, liquorice sticks, cough candy, boiled sweets, dolly mixtures, and nut or plain toffee.

On the counter were scales made of brass, a small steel hammer for breaking up the toffee, which Miss Tapp did by placing a piece of toffee in the palm of her hand. She would then hit it sharply with the hammer. Next she formed a paper bag by twisting a square of paper round her hand and twisting the end to make a cone shape. She would ring up the purchases on her ancient cash register and a drawer would shoot open. After she sorted the money and any change, she would push the drawer shut with a bang.

On Saturdays my brother and I would go to the shop to spend our pocket money. Mine was a penny and I usually chose a 'hap'orth' of dolly mixtures and a halfpenny toffee bar.

One Saturday three boys came into the shop for their sweets. 'What would you like?' said Miss Tapp in a cheerful voice to the first boy.

He wanted a pennyworth (he said penn'orth) of bulls' eyes. Miss Tapp took the steps and climbed up to reach the sweets, weighed out the bulls 'eyes, put the jar back on the top shelf, gave the boy his sweets and took his penny.

'Do you want something?' she asked the second boy.

'Yes please, Miss Tapp. I'd like a penn'orth of bulls' eyes too.'

So she went up the steps again for the sweet jar, weighed them, and before she put the jar back, Miss Tapp said to the third boy, 'I suppose you want a pennyworth of bulls' eyes too?'

'No,' replied the boy. So again she took the sweet jar and placed it back on the shelf.

'What do you want, then?,' she asked the third boy – in an irritated voice.

'I only want a hap'orth of bulls' eyes.'

Besoms and Broomsticks
by Olga Tramontin

It had started when her boys were small, the witchy thing. First one would be naughty, or maybe two out of three; usually teasing the third brother. Then baby came along and the three of them ganged up on the precious bundle: nothing really malicious, just a tad of natural jealousy toward the new-born who took up so much of Mum's time. There would be the odd snigger at his mewling, or a whispered 'yuk!' when she changed a soiled nappy: sometimes a pinch from number three son, who had – after all – been the precious one for so long.

When Mum said 'I saw that,' or 'I heard that,' the miscreant would jump back, showing his guilt.

'How did you know, Mum? How did you guess it was me?'

After a while, her 'I just do' became a bit wishy-washy, having been said so often. One day, almost out of frustration, she answered 'because I'm a witch.'

This response appealed tremendously to four growing boys. It explained their getting caught when they did their naughty deeds and at school it became a defence against school bullies. They would yell at their attackers 'Watch it, YOU. My Mum's a witch and she could turn you into a warty frog.'

Mum's mysterious powers encouraged homework to be done on time, because there was always a little reward at the end of each project. A sparkling high bounce ball, a hologram yo-yo, or one of those fluorescent torches that lit up dark rooms so magically, would be there on the tea table when they arrived home from school.

'How did you know I got high marks, Mum?' And before she could say it, 'I know – because you're a witch.'

Thus four boys grew up, comfortable with Mum's witchiness that gave her these special powers to do kindly, amazing and wise things. She was not a wicked witch, not one that you screamed at when you went to a pantomime; she was what was known as a first-class witch, she told them, the best ones in the magic world...

One by one they married, had children of their own. Wonderful babies for a special Grandma to cuddle, to nuzzle into those warm, sweet infant smells. She watched with pride when first one then the next gave her a smile, took their early tottering steps, and said their first words.

Still occasionally she weaved her magic. Laurie, daughter-in-law number three, who was so heavily pregnant and continued to suffer from morning sickness and chronic heartburn complained, 'I shall be so glad to drop this one. I'm so tired of this awful sickness. As for heartburn! Reckon I keep Rennies – and the like – in business.'

'May is nearly over,' cautioned her wise mother-in-law. 'She will be born in June and have lots of hair.'

'How on earth do you know that?'

'Cos I'm a witch,' she said, with a knowing smile and a shrug of her shoulders. Her third granddaughter, Tilly, was born on the first of June with a mop of curly hair...

Number one son travelled east, to seek fame and fortune in exotic foreign climes, with his mother's blessing and a hidden tear. He had been such a comfort to her during his boyhood years, especially after Merlin, her darling man, had died so soon following the precious one's birth.

'You'll be back every year, especially in springtime,' she told him as she waved goodbye. 'The grass is always greener then.'

He sent her regular letters and photos of exotic places and his new, growing family.

Number two son went north, to the lucrative oilfields, in his helicopter. She gently advised him to take care, and silently prayed for his safe return.

'Wish it was your broomstick, Ma,' he had laughed, that lovely special laugh belonging so very much to him, and his deep blue eyes sparkled in their own magic way. 'Then I'd know that I'll be safe.'

Strange winds blew – one black and stormy night – and Jack's helicopter fell out of the sky. She knew when it happened, awoke and paced the room, even before the police knocked at her door in those early hours. Mothers always do, especially the witchy ones.

Number three son went south and became a fine builder, confident he would make a fortune and keep her in luxury forever. He had been allowed to develop a new estate on flood meadows, from where farmers moved their cattle and sheep in winter. 'How did you get permission to construct there?' she asked, even before he had laid any foundations. 'It'll surely be under water by the New Year.'

The farmers drove their cattle and sheep away but Dan could not move his houses when they began to crack and subside. He lost his fortune compensating the buyers of 'Meadow Homes'. He was her philosophical son; he shrugged his shoulders, moved on and built again.

She so admired his courage, proud to see him start once more from nothing. It hardly mattered that he forgot the luxury he had promised. There was no hurry; she could live quite happily without.

Number four son had declared for years, 'I'll stay home, Mum – someone should look after you.'

She argued with him. 'Go out there, son. The world is yours, go see it and enjoy it.'

When he was nineteen Bristol University offered him a place. He and she danced around the room with glee and she told him how delighted she was for him, how proud he had made her. He packed his books, she packed his bags and he kissed her goodbye at the station. 'You'll be ok, won't you Mum?'

'Of course I will, silly. Don't I have my magic to protect me? Go and have fun; meet new people, learn new things.'

She eagerly awaited his letters giving her news of his progress. At Bristol University he met Portia and wrote to his mother to tell her, 'this is the girl I want to marry.'

She imagined her – with that special name – to be tall, willowy, elegant and serene. The first two yes, the latter two no. Tall and willowy, Portia was also colourful and vibrant, not elegant or serene, but witchy 'mother-in-law to be' loved her on sight.

They married, after they both graduated, holding their reception on the beach among fellow students, with a huge bonfire like a beacon and delicious smells of barbecue. In a place of honour, she watched them as they danced on sand and among teasing, shallow waves to the music of guitars, flutes and small hand-held drums. Portia's dress flowed like gossamer as she swirled in the arms of her white-suited husband. Their chocolate wedding cake, in the shape of a galleon, melted in the hot sunshine but it didn't seem to matter.

Two years later, with Portia pregnant, they moved from furnished rooms into their own home. In the back garden they found a besom propped up against the wall.

'See? Mum's taxi,' declared Dryden.

'I don't believe it,' Portia laughed.

'Bet you anything, Mum will be somewhere near: she promised to help us move.'

The doorbell rang.

'I told you so.'

'But how do you know it's her?'

'Cos I'm a warlock.' He grinned.

A Whisper
by Sue Whiting

I thought I heard a noise
It was distant, but it was there,
A whisper, a sigh
Trembling on the midnight air.

Had she come to say goodbye?
Returned from those distant shores?
I saw her – just briefly,
But I knew she could be no more.

She was a visual fallacy,
Had entered the long sleep.
I reached out to gently touch her,
But nothing – I stand and weep.

I weep as I see her pass over.
Is it to the celestial city of love?
Part of me dies with her.
But will she always be above?

Above to watch down over me,
To ease the pain of parting loss?
But my heart is truly broken,
This line I cannot cross.

Until I reach the Stygian shores
I know we'll be apart,
So fare thee well my dearest one
Forever in my heart.

Kentucky Fire
by Rosemarie David

The horse racing industry is riddled with superstition and one particular saying came to mind when Mae-Belle's colt was born. It was a misty morning on the small holding in Kentucky but the barn was warm and the solid bay mare delivered her foal without fanfare. He was a gangly fire red chestnut with four white knee length stockings and a small white flash on his muzzle. Rosie and old Joe looked at each other and their joy was slightly subdued for a moment as the same thought flashed through their minds (four white socks and a snip on the nose, tan his hide and feed him to the crows). What it meant was that white hooves were soft, and having four was a distinct disadvantage for a racehorse.

Red, as he came to be known, had the easy going temperament of his dam and soon became a favourite around the farm. He was Mae-Belle's third foal and it was hoped that it would be third time lucky as although her two previous sons had won a few local races they lacked the stamina required for a Derby winner. Winning the Kentucky Derby was the dream of every owner and trainer. It had been run at Churchill Downs, Louisville, Kentucky since 1875. A left handed dirt track, 10 furlongs (1 and a quarter miles) long for three year old thoroughbreds. With this in mind, Mae-Belle had been put to a stallion with lineage that traced back to the great racehorse Man O War. The stud fee had been more than Rosie could really afford but the resulting colt held all her dreams of winning the Derby. He would be registered and run under the name of Kentucky Fire.

As Red grew he proved to be everything a prospective racehorse should be. He was flashy with his red and white colours and his kind willing temperament soon made him a favourite with all who met him. He ran with great heart over short distances but he flagged on the longer runs so his training was intensified and he won the respect of stable boy and trainer alike as he raced around the track. Always a winner in their eyes: but would he make the grade in the big race.

Time passed and Red was entered in a few local races. He won some and he lost some but Rosie was determined that he would have his victory and the garland of roses that his lineage promised. Old Joe loved that horse and would talk to him for hours about the history of the thoroughbred horse and the thrill of the track. Red nuzzled him and dozed, lulled by the familiar voice and kind hand.

Time passed and Red began to win more and more of his starts. His stamina increased and he became the toned athlete that Rosie expected him to be. She was sure that he had a good chance of winning the Derby. Red's trainer was not so sure and tried to dissuade her from entering him but Rosie said that Red would only have one chance and he deserved the opportunity.

Race day arrived with all the pomp and circumstance expected of such an occasion. Red's coat shone like a new penny and his muscles rippled as he walked around the enclosure with his jockey on board. Although his reputation as a stayer preceded him, the odds were against him, due to superstition and his white feet. Ben leant down from the saddle and whispered encouragement into his ear, then ran a hand lightly down his neck. The horses began to make their way to the gates: some were skittish, but Red just cantered easily along with no signs of stress. The horses were boarded and then the bell rang, and the gates swung open. Horses erupted onto the track amidst screams from the crowd. The commentator's voice echoed over the spectators, naming the runners.

In the middle of the bunch, Kentucky Fire galloped along at a steady pace. Then, suddenly, he dropped back and Ben felt Red's muscles bunch as the big horse began to move around the other runners. Launching himself from the far side, his legs moving like pistons and his hooves kicking up the dust he surged ahead.

Rosie was stunned. Her horse had never shown such strength and speed. Ben rose in his stirrups, holding his whip hand in the air and felt the hot rush of wind in his face. The crowd went mad as the big red horse crossed the finish line lengths ahead of the favourite. Kentucky Fire had won the Derby!

Hold your strength till the barriers fly,
then close with the leaders eye to eye.
Thundering hooves and the mad jammed race,
blood in the nostrils, sweat in the face.
And children, remember wherever you are,
you carry the blood of Man o' War.

Anon

A Holiday to Remember
by Maureen Thomas

Molly's husband heaved the last of the suitcases into the car and sighed with relief. It was the first holiday they had had together for a number of years and he was really looking forward to it. The family had all voted unanimously on a camping holiday in Scotland.

Now they were all ready, four children Amanda, Jane, Sue and the youngest Charlie plus a very excited mongrel dog called Muffin were all squeezed into the car, which was attached to a large trailer tent which almost got left behind because Tom had forgotten to attach it! So one very embarrassed father climbed into the driver's seat.

'Are we ready?' he shouted.

'Yes, we are,' everyone replied.

'Have we got everything?' Tom shouted.

'Yes, we have,' sighed everyone.

'Then where are the car keys?' Tom shouted again. 'Everyone out and start looking for the keys , someone must have seen them.'

Mollie and the children all groaned and got out of the car. For Muffin, it was another chance to pee up the car wheel. Unfortunately, Tom saw him and was about to scold him when he saw the car keys on the ground, 'Oh dear, sorry ,they must have fallen from my pocket while I was trying to stuff all our gear into the car. Ok guys emergency over, all back in the car and we're away.'

They all clambered back in, lots of elbows and knees everywhere, safety belts on, and they were away... AT LAST!

As Tom drove along they all started singing and after a while the hustle and bustle of town life quickly faded into green fields and long country roads. They had been travelling for about two hours when a little voice came from the back seat, 'Mum, I need a wee!' It was Charlie the youngest.

Dad found a service station where they could visit the loos and stretch their legs, they also had a bite to eat and were soon on their way again.

Scotland seemed one heck of a way to a little boy of Charlie's age but they soon crossed the border and the scenery changed dramatically. Tall pine trees, beautiful lochs and rocky mountains. They were soon at the farmhouse where they were staying and pitched their tent, and Mollie began making their first camp site meal of fresh eggs and bacon with beans and toast. After they had finished and all the pots washed and put away, they all took a stroll around the farm.

It was one of those places where you could feed the new born lambs, collect eggs and if you fancied, the farmer's wife would give bread making lessons, doing it the old fashioned way with lots of kneading and stretching and pulling of dough. There was a lot to see on the farm and all the children loved meeting all the animals. After a good look-around they all went back to the tent where a very tired little Charlie was put to bed.

The next day after a hearty breakfast they all went out and, after a short drive, found themselves beside a most beautiful loch. They couldn't resist getting out of the car to explore the area. It was idyllic. The water was so clear and the trees gave a vivid reflection in the calm still water. Molly and Tom sat with their feet dabbling in the water whilst they kept their eyes on the children, who were playing nearby. The sun shone down making the water sparkle like diamonds; there was nothing on earth that could be more beautiful than this they thought. As the days flew by they thought how lucky they were that they could be all together like this.

All too soon it was time to go home: they had had a wonderful week in Scotland, and were very sad to leave. When they were packed up and ready to leave, the farmer's wife gave them eggs and fresh bread and proper farmhouse cheese.

'So that you won't get hungry on the way home,' she said.

The children were very sad to leave the new puppies that had been born while they were there. They were all leaving a piece of their hearts in this wonderful place and shed a few tears before they drove away on that long journey back home.

The Dark Night
by Carol Campbell

It's only dark as long as you allow it to be
Sometimes you need to look for the light within the darkness
To see a direction
And see the way to go.

You need to look for the warmth within the coldness
To melt the moments that are frozen in time
And melt the coldest of hearts
Where there is dark there is light
And where there is light there is darkness.

Every situation and place are both available to the naked eye
But sometimes you have to look within to see the real light.
The spark of light that ignites that little more
To enable it to grow into something much bigger
And better for everyone and everything.

Because you looked into the darkness of the night
And saw and felt the light within.

Compassion
by Rosemarie David

Billy walked slowly towards the dry river bed. His small suntanned hands cradled the dish of bread and milk with care. Small for his age at six, Billy was slender and brown as a berry from the intense African sun. His sandy coloured hair was streaked with blond and his khaki shorts and shirt were faded. Old leather sandals coated in dust held feet scratched by thorns and rocks. Billy was a happy child with a deep love of the outdoors and all animals; he would often bring little mammals needing care home to his Mother. Their home was rural and the only neighbours they saw were the local farm workers who lived nearby. Billy's Father worked on the mines in Zambia and was only home a couple of days every month.

Lowering the dish to the river bed, Billy walked back a few steps and sat on a rock under the Acacia tree. The drought had lasted many months and Billy had been feeding his friend for the past few weeks as there was no food available for the wild creatures.

Slowly a narrow head emerged from a nearby rocky outcrop. The snake emerged and slid towards the dish. He did not look at the boy but went straight to the food and began to eat. Billy watched the cobra as he finished the food and then returned to his nest. Lifting the empty dish, Billy made his way home.

Mary was curious about the friend that Billy needed the food for, but he would not say what the animal was. He shrugged her questions off and just told her his friend was hungry, and she could not meet him as he did not like strangers. Billy knew how dangerous the cobra was and he did not want his Mother to find out about it. One day she decided to follow him. That was the day that her son's compassion was rewarded.

Billy sat under the tree watching the snake eat. Suddenly it turned towards the boy and rising to full height opened its hood. Billy sat frozen as the snake moved towards him. Then it shot forward flying over his shoulder and colliding with the black mamba that had slid unseen down the tree towards the boy. The snakes landed on the ground with a thump, their writhing bodies churning up the dust. Billy jumped up and ran a few feet away from them. Then he stopped and turned to watch the life and death battle. It was over quickly: the cobra slid away from the lifeless body of the mamba and without looking at the boy returned to his nest.

Mary could not stop herself running forward and hugging her son to herself. They were both shaking and crying and she took him home. Billy continued to feed the snake but Mary no longer followed him as she knew he would be safe. A few weeks later the drought broke and the river ran with life giving water again, the grasses and trees brightened up, and the dust turned to mud. Billy cried, because his friend no longer came to eat, but his Mother explained that he had enough to eat now as the tiny mammals had returned.

It was a year later as Billy sat beside the river with his fishing rod that he felt someone watching him and turned his head to look straight into the face of a cobra with its hood open. Billy smiled and turned back to the river. The snake closed its hood and slid around him and over his leg before it rose up to look into his face. Slowly Billy raised his hand and softly stroked the shiny scales. For an instant the snake turned its head and rested it lightly in his cupped hand. Then it turned from him and slid away. Billy never saw the snake again and his Mother told him that it had come to thank him for looking after it during the drought.

Billy's love of reptiles particularly the king cobra began with that unusual friendship when he was just a young boy. He grew up to become a ranger with the Wankie National Park in Rhodesia and continued to work with and care for animals for the rest of his life.

A Walk Through the Woods
by Carol Campbell

I was so glad of the company as I walked down the winding path that led through the woods. The trees whispered as if they were having a hushed conversation. I strained to listen but couldn't quite hear.

I smiled at my walking companion as we trekked further on into the woods. 'Hark at them,' I said.

James chuckled. 'I often talk to the trees,' he said. 'I sometimes think they're the only ones who understand me.'

I looked at him and giggled. 'Do you come here often?' I said.

James smiled a wide grin, his brilliant white teeth glistening in the fast approaching dusk. 'You could say that, Charlotte. It's on my way home. I like to think after finishing work, plus I enjoy the open space and listening to the sounds of the wild. It makes you appreciate how lucky we are: how we should value nature maybe that little bit more.'

'I agree with you, totally,' I said.
'And you know, James. I would never normally walk with a stranger, but I do feel quite safe walking with you.'

James smiled. 'That's one thing you are, lovely Charlotte: safe with me and safe with nature. I've walked this route for years, and I'll make sure you get to the crossroads safely. When you see the farmhouse, you'll know where you are and you'll be fine.'

Just then an owl hooted. I stood still. James stopped and looked at me. 'You all right, love?'

'Yes, I'm fine. Isn't that sound simply beautiful?'

'Yes love, it is. Can you hear the wings beating?'

I strained my ears. 'Wow, that's amazing.'

Suddenly there was a whoosh sound as the owl swooped through the trees at a super-fast speed.

'He missed,' said James. 'Better luck next time.'

I smiled at James as I caught up with him. 'Almost there,' he said.

I could see a faint light in the distance that just seemed to grow, almost like the rising sun at daybreak.

As we got nearer, James started to whistle a little ditty. Then suddenly the light, the farmhouse, and cross-roads were straight in front of us. James had stopped whistling. I turned to thank him, but he had gone – I was alone.

'James,' I called out, but there was no reply. 'Where has he gone?' I spoke out loud.

As I knocked on the farmhouse door, the lady who opened the door said, 'Hi Charlotte. You found it ok then?'

'Yeah,' I said. 'But this guy walked with me and now he's vanished.'

Cath looked at me and asked, 'What did he look like?'

'Well he looked a bit like an old farmer, and he whistled.'

Cath smiled. 'James has been at it again. He was my great grandfather. He has a habit of turning up when he's needed. You're not the first person he's walked through the woods; he does it all the time.'

'Well,' she continued. 'Don't just stand there with your mouth open love, come on in and shut the door.'

As I closed it behind me I could have sworn I heard the trees laughing in the distance.

Great Uncle Carey
by Olga Tramontin

He was larger than life as he sat in his giant's chair. Great Uncle Carey was a big man, with thick white wavy hair, bushy eyebrows and a magnificent curling moustache. His smile displayed long teeth and twinkling blue eyes. He had a boomer of a voice, quite awesome to a four year old.

His library, overlooked vast lawns, with trees that were easy to climb. Except for the monkey puzzle tree whose leaves were very sharp. The lawns led down to a dry-stone wall, with a steep incline beyond that Uncle Carey called a 'haha', because you couldn't see the incline until you came upon it.

We used to stroll around the garden most afternoons.

'I planned it,' he said. 'So there'd be flowers blooming every month throughout the year.'

'Even in winter?' I asked.

'Certainly. In December the hellebores bloom, followed by January snowdrops and spring daffodils, bluebells, crocuses and tulips. Come May the summer flowers bloom right through to autumn. Then I plant cyclamen and winter-flowering pansies to fool old Jack Frost,' and he would laugh his loud, booming laugh.

He could easily have been Father Christmas: not the real one of course, but better than the department store ones that Ma took me to see until I grew too old to believe in Santa. I did, however, have a sneaking regard for Tolkien's Hobbit which Uncle Carey read to me. I would climb up on his lap and snuggle beneath his arms as he held the book. That way I could see the pictures. His voice, though, was so expressive there was little need for illustrations, and I believed he could talk in hobbit voices.

Such a happy childhood I had with this wonderful man. Great Uncle Carey never married, never had children, but regarded my mother as his daughter, not his niece. I suppose he thought of me as his grandson. To me he was the father I never knew, mine being killed during the Falklands War.

One day Great Uncle Carey took ill. He coughed a lot leaving red spots on his large white handkerchief. We spent more time in the library, him in his red leather chair and me at his feet as he read or slept. We no longer walked outdoors, such exertion bringing on coughing spasms and more red spots on his handkerchiefs. He grew thin, his thick hair became sparse, even his moustache drooped in sadness. Later he took to his bed, a huge four-poster with muslin drapes that he said discouraged mosquitoes.

'I've never seen mosquitoes in England,' I told him.

'Ah,' he replied. 'They can still be there lurking.'

He began taking his meals in bed, pappy, easily digested food. He grew weaker and could no longer hold books: I read them aloud instead. He especially liked Sherlock Holmes stories: also the American writer, John Steinbeck. I preferred him to Sir Arthur Conan Doyle. Steinbeck reminded me of Uncle Carey, how he described people and places, bringing them alive.

One morning my mother said, 'Don't go into Uncle Carey's room.'

'Why not?' I asked.

'Because... I'm afraid, my darling, he died in his sleep last night.'

I cried bitterly and refused to go to school that day, wanting only to sit with the old man, tell him I loved him: read to him, anything. But Ma wouldn't let me.

'Wait till the nurse visits,' she said. 'She'll make him look nice, then you can see him.'

With that I had to be content. He was buried a week later in our village churchyard; in springtime when daffodils and bluebells waved him farewell. I stood by his graveside in my grown-up black suit and said goodbye to a beloved great uncle. Later my mother told me he had left his entire library to me, including his red leather chair. The house he bequeathed to my mother.

I sat in that chair and gazed through the window onto the lawns and down to the haha, holding a special edition of Steinbeck's 'The Wayward Bus'.

It was signed 'To my dear friend, Carey, remembering our journey through America. Best wishes J.S.'

My tears washed the pages as I remembered my dear friend, Great Uncle Carey.

Forgive
by Carol Campbell

Forgiveness can be a hard subject to approach
But at the same time it can be the easiest
It's a way of letting go
And releasing a burden
That has weighed you down for far too long

Being angry takes up valuable energy
As does being bitter
It's you the pain effects
Not the perpetrator
Or the reason you're angry

They may think they're never wrong
By forgiving it doesn't make them right
But it does mean you're no long prepared
To carry the pain
That they put to rest on your shoulders.

So release it, like letting the balloon go,
And feel at peace with yourself.

The Good Luck Tree
by Liz Penn

Although dirty and tired Jacob knew he would have to walk. He had ridden his horse hard and fast, and the stallion had been strong and full of energy, but the heat and lack of food and water had made the horse stumble and fall. Jacob knelt beside him and stroked his mane, then he realised that his front fetlock was horribly twisted and it was obvious the horse had broken his leg. He felt tears stinging his eyes: he had had enough bloodshed and battle, and now having to shoot his horse who was his friend was one act he didn't want to happen.

Jacob was a union soldier who had left Fort Monroe four days earlier. Fort Monroe, located in Virginia, was deep in Confederate territory but was still held by the Union Army. Jacob had arrived there with a company sergeant and was escorting four prisoners. They had travelled from Fredericksburg near where the fighting had been hell, and after saying his goodbyes at Fort Monroe, Jacob had been heading back to General Grant's home town. Now he realised in this year of 1863 he was a lone Union soldier on foot and deep in Confederate territory.

Meanwhile a farmer called Charlie Anderson, lived nearby with his four sons who helped him on the farm. Also his daughter Ann and daughter-in-law, Mary, who helped with the house work. The family had no slaves and Charlie's eldest son Henry wanted to join the war, but Charlie repeatedly told his family 'They wouldn't join the war until it concerned them.' So it came to pass that this elderly farmer discovered a Union soldier asleep in his barn.

Eventually peace came to this war torn Country, and in summer time in the year of 1865, a lone rider left a farm where he had been a captive for two long years. The son of a preacher, Jacob had had a good education, married at the age of 23 years, and then only spending two weeks with his young bride, he had enlisted and went off to war.

Jacob had worked hard for Charlie, turning his hand to any menial task given him, they all knew there was no way of him getting home, so he had worked and prayed, and realised it was better living on Charlie's farm than facing the horrendous battles he had been part of.

Three months after leaving Virginia, a weary man rode his horse into the village of Gallini, he was just another Union soldier coming home after four long years.

He'd almost forgotten her, and what she looked like. Was she still there? Jacob turned his horse around and trotted along the leafy lane. He didn't see her right away, just the tree, the big old oak tree, and then the yellow ribbon tied round the tree, and the words came back to him. 'Tie a yellow ribbon round the old oak tree, three long years since you have married me.'

Golden curls bouncing off her shoulders and hitching up her skirts she was running towards him. 'I never gave up Jacob. I knew you would come home, that's why I left the yellow ribbon round the 'ole oak tree', and it brought GOOD LUCK.

Mr Pratt
by Phyl Furniss

My husband and I hadn't lived in Telford very long. We'd moved from a flat to a new three-bedroomed house and were now able to invite the family to stay. Our daughter, Dinah, and her two children, Janet, seven and Martin, four, were invited for the weekend as Bob, her husband, was away on business in America.

It was a lovely summer's day as they set off. Their journey would take about an hour. They were driving along the M6 when a large car cut across Dinah's. Her reaction was to lift one hand and shout after the driver as he sped past them along the motorway.

'Who was that man you waved to, Mum? Do you know him?' asked Martin. 'Was his name Pratt?'

To keep her son happy Dinah answered, 'Yes, Martin, he's Mr Pratt and he works in Grandpa's office.'

This satisfied young Martin and the incident seemed to be forgotten. They arrived at our house in time for lunch. Martin jumped out of the car and ran down the path.

'Grandpa, Grandpa,' he shouted to his grandfather who waited to greet them at the front door. 'We saw a friend of yours on the motorway.'

'Did you Martin, who was that?'

'Mr Pratt, and Mum said he works in your office.'

With a twinkle in his eye Grandpa asked a red faced Dinah what she had been telling her young son about his 'friend', Mr Pratt.

Never Give Up Hope
by Carol Campbell

There's always a light in the distance
But we do need to keep the faith
That the light will grow
And glow long enough
For our strained eyes to see
So long as there's hope there's a chance
And as long as there's a chance there's hope
So never give up hope
Even if it's all you have for a moment
That moment may become reality
Where you no longer have to hope
Because that dream just came true.

I Had No Idea
Ruth Broster

When I was very young I had no idea about the subject of geography until high school, even though my parents loved to travel around the country, and as a family we were soon to emigrate to Australia.

You could see my parents were having a great time and they loved each other's company, but they were not really the type of parents who would give you hours of their time especially as an individual to help you learn or study, they kind of left that sort of thing up to yourself to get on with, good manners were more important to them, and we were sometimes told "don't speak until you're spoken to". I would imagine this way of life was due to part of their own upbringing as I am sure we all have mum and dad in us and pass it down along the way.

Mum loved company, more adult rather than children although she had quite a few, eight of us to be precise, she did say to me when I got older and had my own children that she just kept having babies as she felt lost without the handles of the pram or pushchair in front of her until the day my father said "enough's enough."

I do recall a time when my father actually listened to what I had to say. It was the time of the early Cindy and Tressy doll days, all the girls seem to have one except me. I had a very cheap imitation Cindy but I didn't mind in the slightest as she had lots of hair that I could style which gave me great pleasure for hours on end. Then the Cindy and Tressy wardrobe came out and there was no chance of me having one of those, so one day when my father was working inside his shed doing up old lawn mowers, a hobby of his and a way of making a little extra cash on the side as wages were very low. I thought, dare I ask him to make me a dolls' wardrobe or will he bite my head off for asking? I finally picked up the courage to ask and low and behold he was agreeable. Yes! He made me a beautiful little dolls' wardrobe out of some old plywood that was knocking around in the shed as dad would never throw anything away. I can see now why I am a bit of a hoarder, never throwing anything away too, in case it comes in handy, the worst gene ever to inherit, as now, I have to try hard to de-clutter when things get too much.

After realising my father would take the time to listen, I decided at a later date to ask him if I could have some books as I adored pictures as well as the words. I also wanted to learn so much about the world. He smiled and said if he could sell the next lawn mower he would take me to a jumble sale and buy me a book. Well, you can imagine how chuffed I was at this.

My parents were both out one day and this couple came to the house having just seen the lawn mower advertisement in the local newspaper shop window. I gave them a demonstration on some long grass that my father kept at the bottom of the garden especially for this reason. I also managed to do a pretty good job with my sales pitch he had taught me. I made a sale of ten shillings, all at the age of nine. Mum and Dad were over the moon.

My father took me to a jumble sale just as he promised and I came away with a book about world history, a book about the Queen Mother and a pair of tap dancing shoes all for less than a shilling.

At this stage in my life I did struggle a bit with my reading as I had poor eye sight. It carried on through my life without me really knowing till my late twenties when I decided to learn to drive. I loved the books so much and the pictures were so beautiful, and one thing in particular always stood out in my mind and that was a tribal man sitting on the back of a huge turtle. I was so fascinated as all I had was a tiny little tortoise, and seeing something like this was amazing.

After arriving in Australia, at first I found it very difficult settling down into a new high school as they seemed to be more advanced in education and yet far behind in everything else: it was more like the early fifties than the late sixties. Knowing one of the subjects was going to be geography, well you can guess how I would feel, I was in my glory, but I am sad to say I never learnt a thing as most of the other children were not interested in geography and made it so difficult for me to learn, apart from how to throw paper aeroplanes and how to be cheeky to the teachers, and fight with each other or be bullied if you didn't participate. Well, what a let-down.

As you know, life goes on and many things happen and change, but here I am now aged fifty eight, children all grown up and fled the nest, and more time on my hands, so I am going to look after number one.

Believe in You
by Carol Campbell

The most important person to believe in
Is yourself
Don't start to doubt yourself because someone doesn't agree with you
Don't change your mind because others tell you to.
Trust yourself
And believe that your feelings and emotions are important
Because they are.

And you are capable of anything
Including succeeding
Because you believed what you thought and felt mattered
Because it does.
And when you believe in yourself
You will soon find many more people
Will also believe in you.

The Shack
by Sue Whiting

They had been walking along the dirt track for about thirty minutes. They felt really worried about breaking down in the outback, with no houses for miles. But they saw a sign saying Shack I Km, so they followed the path. They could see it in the distance and felt quite relieved. But as they got closer, they could see how run down it was. There were two rusting old cars out the front.

Jan knocked on the wooden door but, as she did so, she could tell it wasn't locked. They slowly went inside calling out all the time, 'Anybody there?' Surely there was someone to help them?

It was the smell they noticed first. They had a look round to see if there was a phone. They did find a mobile on the dusty old sideboard, but its battery was completely flat. They looked around for a landline, but it was obvious there wasn't one.

They saw a few rucksacks on the floor that somehow seemed out of place. Now they were in the middle of the outback with no way of getting help. They thought, if they waited a while, perhaps the owner might return, might be able to help them somehow.

Soon it started to get dark. They found a little rusting oil lamp which they managed to light, but it wasn't much good at piercing the gloom. It was then they heard the noise. Suddenly the door blew open and their screams were lost in the night. Then silence.

'Look, there's a car up ahead,' said Kora. 'Perhaps they've broken down.'

'We really should get more water from somewhere,' said Jenny.

'There's a sign up there.' Kora squinted at it. ' It says shack 1Km. Let's try up there, they're bound to have some water.'

They knocked on the wooden door, found it unlocked. They entered, calling out. It was the smell that repulsed them...

All That Glitters is not Gold
by Liz Penn

He gently prized the rock up and underneath noticed how muddy the soil appeared to be. Ron wiped his brow, thinking that the rock would have been a lot harder to move than it had been but for the torrential rain and thunder storms that must have loosened it in the week.

The old man had asked him to be a good son and turn over the soil on his allotment. In this year of 1947 there were still food shortages, and he wanted to plant some lettuces and radishes and spring onions. He had complained to Ron that his rheumatism was making it difficult to bend. So, like the good son he was, Ron had come over to help him out, ignoring the 1001 jobs he had at home waiting for his attention.

It was just an impulse that had made him remove the rock and now, as he tossed it to one side, he raked the thick muddy soil and suddenly felt and heard something hitting the rake. Ron thought initially that it must be a piece of glass, then as he bent down to look he realised that it was a coin of sorts, then he noticed other coins, in fact he found four, of which all looked very old, and with their markings almost erased.

Suddenly, he became aware of other raised voices and he noticed several men on the other allotments had stopped what they were doing and were waving and shouting to him. Ron gathered up his new found treasures and walked over to them. Surprise, surprise: they had also found coins, and a lot more than Ron's four.

After much discussion Alf, the younger one of the three gardeners, suggested he take them to the local antiques shop to see what value they had, and an agreement was made that they would all meet in the local pub at eight o'clock to see what they were worth, and to share and spend the proceeds.

Ron finished his weeding and digging and went in to see his Dad and tell him about their find of a treasure haul of immense value. The old

45

man listened intently to Ron, finally nodding and smiling said, 'Let me tell you my story, Ron. For many years I collected coins, any ones I could lay my hands upon. It became an obsession with me and there were times when I even took the odd one or two that I saw lying about. I collected them in a tall tin, and up until a few weeks ago I still had them, but I was so short of money lad, so three weeks ago I took them down to that antiques shop for a valuation. The dealer examined them pretty closely, one by one, and told me they were worthless, absolutely worthless: wouldn't even buy a packet of fags.'

Ron hid a smile and said, 'What happened then, Dad?'

'Well, on the night I got home from the dealer, I went over to the allotments and chucked the lot away: a handful here, a handful there. But when I came to my plot I only had four left, so I wedged them under the rock.'

Ron listened to his story and exclaimed,' What an old Devil you are. I tell you what: from now on, go and do your own digging, cos I'm finished.' He reached for his coat, and walked out. However, there was a little smile playing on his lips as he walked away. But he too had his thoughts of 'if only' – like his Dad must have had previously.

A Place in the Outback
by Maureen Thomas

Bruce was a humble sixty four year old man, with dark brown eyes and copper hair. He could be stubborn at times and scared of failure. So why should he find himself in this God forsaken place in the middle of nowhere? This was the Australian outback and as far as Bruce was concerned it was unfamiliar, hot, very dry and most unwelcoming. He blamed his wife Maggie for his predicament: she was always telling him that he should be more adventurous and try new things.

Since her untimely death two years previously, Bruce had found it very difficult to be adventurous and had hardly ventured out, he wished now that he had been a little more outgoing for her sake and he really did feel that he had failed her. They used to take regular holidays, always staying in the same country, but it had continuously been Maggie's dearest wish to have a place in the Australian outback where they could REALLY get away from the stresses and strains of city life. She wanted to go where no-one else was likely to be.

"There's certainly no-one here Maggie,' he said aloud, as if she was sitting beside him.

He was feeling even more lonely now: today would have been their wedding anniversary. It had taken him a long time to pluck up the courage to come here and he thought he was mad to go through with all the plans and preparations without her love and support.

As he sat there day dreaming in the intolerable heat, an empty glass of beer in his hand, his eyes slowly closed and his mind drifted back to the first time they had met. They had both been in their early fifties. It was on the internet they met, a chance photograph, a nervous first date. In fact they had spent that day just talking and laughing, it felt like he had known her for ages.

At his time of life he never dreamed of falling in love, but he had, and it felt wonderful! Bruce just wanted Maggie to be part of his life and after a respectable time, they were married in his local village church. It was a simple but beautiful occasion. As they stood to take their vows his eyes wondered at her beauty and it was at that moment he knew that he would spend the rest of his life trying to make Maggie happy...

Life was idyllic until Maggie started to feel unwell, always tired, feeling sick and she was definitely not her usual bubbly self. It was not long after their first wedding anniversary that the doctor gave them the news that they didn't want to hear.

Maggie had leukaemia and had only months to live. Of course, Bruce blamed himself and wondered where he had gone wrong. They went away and tried to live with what time they had left together. At first they went on short breaks away but not too far. But it was still Maggie's dearest wish to visit the Australian outback. Sadly, she never made it.

Bruce fell asleep in the hot sun, still holding his empty glass in his right hand... Maggie stood before him and held his other hand. She was looking straight into his eyes and was telling him that she was happy now that they had made it to Australia and that everything would be ok, they were living their dream.

Bruce was woken by a loud buzzing of a large fly that was trying to salvage something from the bottom of his beer glass. When he looked up, he realised that the woman he had loved so dearly had gone from his life, but he now knew that he had done the right thing in coming here and he had helped to fulfil her dream of a place in the outback.

Wow What A Holiday
by Carol Campbell

The golden sand melted between my toes, as I walked across the golden beach: the sun blazed down, but it was a comfortable heat. I heard the faint breeze whispering, and I saw the sea was gentle as the foamy surf washed up on the shore. I walked for what seemed to be a long time, but time on my watch stood still, almost static. I was alone or so I thought – you know that feeling when you know someone is there even though they're not.

I heard a giggle, an almost childlike giggle, that took me back to my own childhood and the last holiday I had with my brother. I was six, he was five, and the memories were chasing me; but they actually felt like they had caught me. As I looked down I noticed two shadows walking across the sand, but I'm alone, I thought. Just then I heard the words 'but I'm never far away, and I've never been far away.' I thought to myself, now you're being silly, this is your imagination playing games.

As I carried on walking I saw yet another shadow, one with a partially bandaged leg. 'Nan,' I said then thought 'here we go again'. First Graham, now my Nan: now I'm definitely losing the plot. But sometimes it's nice to have your mind play tricks on you. I almost said this aloud too. Listen my girl, does your mind really play you up this much? My heart jumped so much it almost jumped out of my body. I turned around but no one was there. I thought it better if I sit down and rest for a while.

I was watching the sea, the to-ing and fro-ing of the waves, almost like watching a cradle rocking, and the golden sunshine still smiled down. Even though I was alone, again it didn't feel like I was, I even felt like someone had wrapped their arms around my shoulders.

In the distance I could see a small white and brown dog, with a docked tail wagging, then another dog a similar shape but a little taller, with sticking up ears. This one had a tail and it was wagging nineteen times to the dozen. They were heading straight towards me and I heard a growl. When I think back, I used to have a dog who talked by growling.

I got to my feet, but immediately nearly tripped over. 'You daft bugger Bruce,' I cursed and heard the familiar sneezing which he did when he thought himself amusing. He found a lot amusing, apart from himself getting wet. I stopped in my tracks – thinking 'now you are being stupid.' Bruce had passed to the rainbow bridge seven years ago. Just then a faint spray of rain started to tickle me as it fell all around me. The rain was a mass of colours: golds, purples and blues. It was then I noticed a rainbow stretching above me, hitting the ground just feet away from me.

It was then I heard the alarm and woke up. Later, putting the radio on in the kitchen, the words sang out 'whenever you need me, all you have to do is dream,' Wow, what a holiday, what a dream: sun, sea, and sand, and so much from the past, and now our song, the one Graham and I always sang, 'All you have to do is dream' – or was it just a dream?

The Final Journey
by Rosemarie David

Annabelle held her friend close and a tear trickled down her cheek and fell onto his furry face. He had been a gift from her Grandparents on the day she was born and had been by her side every day for the past 80 years. Today she would decide his future, in an hour she was due at her lawyer's office to finalise her will. She had agonised over her decision, her Granddaughters did not want him although they would welcome the money he could be sold for - she could not bear the thought of him passing from collector to collector – just sitting on a shelf - unloved.

Teddy had soaked up many childish tears: listening to tales of boyfriends and parties. He had felt her hugs of joy when she told him that she was getting married and when her daughter was born: the tears of heartbreak when her husband, her soul mate died. Yes, Teddy was her friend. He had shared her life through good and bad. Annabelle knew that the problem of his future had never really existed as her decision had already been made in her heart – she just had to acknowledge it.

At her funeral four years later, as Annabelle's family and friends stood around the open casket to say their final farewells, some were surprised to see tucked into her side, his face resting against her breast, a large well-loved Steiff teddy bear. The button in his ear gleamed; his black boot button eyes gazed sightlessly ahead and although his mohair was worn and threadbare in places from the fierce hugs he had received over the past 84 years his black stitched smile ~~were~~ was as wide as ever. Annabelle and Teddy would continue their journey as they had always been.~ together .

Sisters by Chance, Friends by Choice
by Liz Penn

Amelia sat on the bus deep in thought. The manager of the supermarket had agreed to let her have tomorrow free if she agreed to go in for the evening next day. Christmas was always a busy time so too much time off wasn't allowed.

Amelia had agreed to that, and this arrangement would give her a chance to see her sister Melanie. It had been two long years since Mom had passed away, and then there had been the argument, the cruel words said to each other; admittedly they were both broken hearted at the time, but the accusations had been unkind.

Melanie had accused Amelia of not looking after Mom when she was so poorly, and Amelia had accused Melanie of only caring for herself and of living the high life, without a caring thought for anyone else at all. Now after all this time her sister was coming to pay a visit for the day. Amelia couldn't help but wonder what the outcome would be as she alighted from the bus, her thoughts were racing.

Six thirty and Amelia was ready, having cooked a delicious pasta bolognaise. There was red wine and Melanie's favourite fresh fruit Pavlova: Amelia hoped it was still her favourite, who knows? She might have changed in the past two years.

Presently there was a loud buzz from the doorbell and Amelia knew her sister had arrived. She opened the door and their arms were round each other in a fond embrace. Amelia stepped back and then could not believe what she was looking at. Was this her well-dressed posh sister?

Flowers decorated her ear lobes, a crochet skull cap sat on her head, plus flowered cotton trousers with a vee at the knee and then coming out in great flares, poncho round her shoulders, and a fashionable patch bag made of many material squares.

Wow, what had happened to Melanie's wonderful dress sense, the leather court shoes, the smart suit and the gorgeous handbag, with super accessories? 'It's flower power, Amelia. I've changed my ways... and come to my senses.' With that, she walked in and apologised to her sister for two years of non-communication.

The evening passed well, and the sisters were the best of friends, all animosity brushed to one side. They hardly stopped to eat as the memories flooded back. Amelia still couldn't get over Melanie's new dress attire, and was told by her sister that she now lived in a commune with many others, all flower power: she no longer worked in a solicitor's office but managed to get by. Amelia didn't understand what the 'get by' meant, but decided not to ask.

After a good night's sleep the sisters sorted out papers, photographs, and documents. They still had many laughs about childhood days and their Mom, then it was time for goodbyes, and the promise of seeing each other much more often. Amelia waved until the taxi disappeared out of sight, then thought, 'Well I had better get ready for work.' Sitting down, she pulled on her black fishnet tights, her mini skirt felt a little tight after all that food the night before, then on went her orange sweater. She looked in the mirror and added a little more gel to her orange hair and managed to spike it just a touch more. With heavily-jewelled fingers Amelia adjusted her nose ring and secured one of her many earrings, and said to herself, as she left for work, 'Flower power... who on earth wants to dress like that?'

The Rose Garden
by Phyl Furniss

The trip by coach to Austin Roses had been planned for several weeks. The day of the trip dawned cool for early summer. Hopefully it would warm up later. They arrived mid-morning and it was decided they would have a coffee break before proceeding into the beautiful gardens.

They sat at small tables, chatting and drinking. Jane, Emma and Anne had been friends for many years, and enjoyed days out together. Anne had lost her husband several years ago and was making the best of her life alone, but it wasn't easy.

Eventually the party started to drift outside. Part of the garden was divided off by small box hedges, designed to suit all tastes, both in layout and the variety of rose trees. The scent from the roses filled the air, the colours were delightful, deep reds to delicate pinks, orange to pale yellows.

The sun came out and its warmth and light made the whole garden come to life. The three of them came across an arbour and Anne decided to sit and take in the beauty surrounding her. June and Emma said they would go on and made arrangements to meet up with Anne later and have lunch.

Anne sat quietly, her thoughts going back to the happy times she had spent with her husband in their little cottage called 'Cuddly Wrens Nest'. There were so many beautiful flowers in their garden, and roses grew in abundance.

There was a well in the front garden and Anne remembered making a wish as she dropped a coin down, hearing the splash as it hit the water below. But that was many moons ago: her wish had been granted then, but now she must look to the future.

Suddenly she heard a voice. 'Why do you look so sad on such a lovely day, and in such a beautiful place?'

Anne looked up and saw a man, smartly dressed in casuals. He had a good head of grey hair and his dark brown eyes twinkled.

'Do I?' she replied. 'I was deep in thought.'

'I'll give you a penny for them,' said the man.

'Oh I don't think you'd really want to know.' There was a smile on Anne's face as she replied.

'You certainly have chosen a lovely spot. May I sit down?'

They sat and chatted: he had lost his wife about the same time Anne had lost her husband, and they found they had many things in common. Suddenly Anne remembered she had to meet up with Jane and Emma for lunch. 'I'll have to go,' Anne said. 'It's been lovely meeting you,' and she hurried away.

Had it all been a dream, or had he really met a charming lady that he would like to meet again? When he reached the restaurant, Anne was already seated at a table with her companions. He looked around for a vacant table but everyone seemed to be occupied, except for a spare chair at Anne's table. He hurried over.

'May I?' he asked politely, pulling the chair out from under the table. 'Of course,' replied Emma.

'You're welcome,' said Jane.

Anne blushed. What should she say? She wasn't going to tell Emma and Jane about her encounter with this man. She looked at him and smiled. He introduced himself as Jim.

'I'm Emma, this is Jane and Anne.'

'Delighted to meet you all,' Jim said and made himself at home with the ladies. 'Have you ordered yet?'

'Not yet,' Jane answered, and they all decided on their meal and placed their orders. Anne glanced at Jim several times and he smiled.

The meal was served and, for a short while, all conversation stopped. Then Jim enquired where they were all returning to.

Emma told Jim exactly where they lived and asked if he knew the place.

'As a matter of fact I live only a couple of miles away from there, I know the place well.'

The meal finished, the coach party was getting ready to leave. The driver was waiting and everyone seemed to move together. Emma and Jane left Anne and Jim together and headed towards the coach.

'Thanks for not letting on we had met earlier.'

Jim took her hand. 'Please let me take you for a meal.'

They arranged a time and place for later that week, and Anne gave Jim her address. He was to pick her up from home.

On the way back, Anne found herself wondering if she had done the right thing, and consequently she had rather a sleepless night.

The following day a box arrived. Inside was a beautiful red rose and a card, which read, 'For the lovely lady in the rose garden.' And, 'See you again soon.'

How lovely, thought Anne. Perhaps my lonely days are over? At least I can enjoy his friendship. Who knows where it may lead?

Birth and all That
by Louise McClean

In my opinion, parenthood is the world's greatest step into the unknown, because you have absolutely no idea what to expect.

The miracle has happened and you are pregnant. Hurrah! You and your husband/partner have read all the books and dutifully attended all the antenatal classes. You have listened carefully to all the professionals who have told you what to expect during the birth – and all that panting! You know the advantages of breast milk and you can safely change a nappy. So, technically you are all set to go – or so you think.

Sadly, the reality is that nothing is quite as you expect. You have been waddling around like an elephant for the past month and you can't wait to become a Mum.

When the labour pains start in earnest your husband goes into panic mode and, by some miracle, actually gets you to the hospital. He is supposed to be calming you down but, in my opinion, it's the other way round.

Now you are in a little room in the hospital and it's been confirmed that this is not a rehearsal and you can't change your mind: you are in at the deep end.

All night long, the midwife keeps coming and going, prodding and poking you, and calmly telling you how you are progressing. Your husband has been massaging your aching back, saying encouraging things, and yawning a lot.

You, on the other hand, have moaned and groaned – or yelled, according to what type of person you are – and greedily gulped at the gas and air. You may also have sworn at your long-suffering husband, blamed him for getting you into this trouble, and have vowed this is to be your one and only child.

However, all that is forgotten once the baby is born. You have given birth to the most beautiful baby in the world and you love your husband again. Together you gaze at this wonderful miracle and can't believe that you really are its parents.

While in hospital you get the hang of breast-feeding, or don't, as the case may be. It's not nearly as easy as you expected, but now it's time to take baby home.

During the short journey home, the baby sleeps – of course – and you put him into the room you have lovingly prepared for him. You sit down and have a cup of tea, prepared by Daddy. Enjoy it; the peace won't last long.

I honestly believed that with a new baby you bathed it, changed it, fed it, winded it, and it went straight off to sleep – while you got on with all the other hundred things you had to do.

But it's not like that at all, because baby never sleeps for longer than half an hour, at the most, so you never get a good sleep either. Sometimes you go around like a zombie all day, never actually getting out of your dressing gown.

You might think, often, that you are no good at breast-feeding so, in desperation, you give the baby a bottle and then feel guilty and a failure, though baby sleeps longer. Good news all round.

And it can take forever to get you and baby ready to leave the house, because now you have to take a car full of baby needs with you: nappies, bottles, creams, a change of clothing.

Often, it doesn't seem worth the bother: it takes longer to prepare to go out than you are actually out. However, believe it or not, you do find some sort of routine eventually and you enjoy showing off your baby to adoring friends and relatives.

You don't bother to mention all the effort it takes, and all the time that you smell of sick on your shoulder: these are overtaken by your pride. The first smile is the best day of your life.

Surely the worst is all behind you. All you have to worry about now is teething, learning to walk and talk, temper tantrums, potty training, pre-school club, and starting school. Next, it's teenage troubles, exams, finding a job or university, girl or boy friends and the heartbreaks, sex, drugs and smoking. Later, you worry that your child should marry the right person. And, before you realise, it's baby time again! Where have the years gone?

With my experience, I say, 'Enjoy it; there's nothing like it.'

Ghost Train
by Carol Campbell

As I stand in the smoggy road an eerie silence begins to approach, The smog is chasing and falling from the above clouds, touching me, and surrounding me until finally hitting the ground.

As I peer across what was once green-belt land, I notice a misty shape in the distance. I smell burning coal and watch as it rises and collides with the smog of the dusty evening sky.

The figure is fast approaching, sounding out rickety-rack as it races nearby. The sounds are echoing out, as if by the face of a cave. Sounding out repeat, repeat, repeat.

Soon the shape is extremely close as it runs along what I thought was once a disused track. There's a hedge standing directly in front of its approach, then nothing,

I look into the space… it's empty… then silence. The hedge stands undamaged, no trace of this mighty wagon of steam. I look at the remains of the track where it hits this space then disappears.

There's a road built the other side, but this side is orange with rust which bounces up to catch my glance.

This track hasn't been used in years.

Stella's Haven
by Ruth Broster

This poem is about my dear late mother in-law Stella who was a keen gardener. She won small garden of the year many times between 1987 and 1999 sponsored by *The Bridgnorth Journal*, *Garden News*, *Shropshire Star Roses & Shrubs* and *Shropshire Star & Bridgemere Garden World*.

Spring could never come too soon
in Stella's eyes its like the month of June
crocuses blooming all around
any excuse for her to be down on the ground
With the blackbird a calling, she'll never miss a tune
for Stella is one with nature and all that's abloom
Listen! she would always say
do you hear that woodpecker, he's been here all day

For never a moment could pass her by
she would always notice something with her keen eye
it may have been the Robin bobbing along
she was always ready to hear his sweet song,

No worm nor weevil can stand in her way
she's up with the lark, even on a rainy day
trowel in her hand with wellie boots too
we can't keep up with her for she's one of a few,
With winter arriving not far ahead
Stella will be out there digging up the bed
to keep them bulbs warm and cosy too
ready for next year to start anew,

You can't help but love her, Stella is like heaven above
for all she ever did was give us her love
her smile was always special too
it's something she would share, with me, and with you,

She may be gone, but it's not for long
just look at the flowers and hear the bird song

then you will know that Stella's about
she wont forget you, without a doubt,
Now! We must not stand in her way
cause knowing Stella
she's here to stay.

The Village Fete
by Rosemarie David

The day was bright and clear and the fete was in full swing. Children were laughing, dogs barking and music blaring, while brightly coloured ribbons hung from the marquees. As Thelma stood looking through her lounge window at the scene on the green her mind drifted to another fete 50 years before.

The sun shone and there was laughter too. The village folk and farmers in the area had all donated what they could to make it a success. There were tea and cupcakes but no chocolate. The white elephant stall boasted handmade items and relics from the attic. Thelma had been helping in the tea tent but she was worried. She had not heard from Simon for a long time or so it seemed to her and she feared the worst.

Suddenly Thelma felt a shiver pass through her and plonking the teapot down on the white cloth she ran toward her home a short distance away. Her senses were jangling. With her long slender legs flying while her skirts flapped about them she ran. She saw the postman coming from her front door his face solemn. 'No' her mind screamed but he passed her by with no comment and she burst through the front door expecting to see a telegram on the floor. Instead his kitbag lay untidily in the hall. Racing to the kitchen with tears of relief pouring down her face Thelma was enfolded in a bear hug. She looked up into a pair of calm grey eyes and then, Simon, in his usual unflappable manner asked

'Would you like a cuppa love I'm gasping'. They both laughed. Had it really been 50 years? How the time had passed by in a whirl of marriage, two beautiful children and everyday activities.

Feeling an arm around her shoulders Thelma looked up into two steady grey eyes and smiled. 'I was remembering' she said softly. Simon hugged her. 'I remember too, sweetheart, but we had better get a move on if we plan to get any tea and cake.' Then hand in hand they walked across the road and towards the green and the village fete.

A Restless Soul
by Maureen Thomas

I lifted the stone carefully and underneath was the key to my past. I was amazed that it was still there after all this time. No one came here anymore and this was my secret. I had lived at the Mansion house with my parents for as long as I could remember, but the house that stood hidden behind the now crumbling stone walls held onto its sad secret and would not let go. I wouldn't let it.

The Mansion used to be a place so full of love and laughter. It was a place where lots of people used to visit, as my parents held regular magical balls in the great hallway. I remember the lights on either side of the drive way, the lovely music and the lively chatter. All the guests arrived in their shiny cars and I remember them all in their finery. These events were such happy occasions. Laughter was everywhere and the events always went on into the early hours.

As I approached the large wooden front door with the rusty key in my hand I looked up to what was once my bedroom window. I could have sworn I saw the curtain twitch, I really did. Gingerly I placed the key into the lock and with a little effort the door creaked open disturbing the enormous spider hiding there in its hinges. I remember the door having the most beautiful carvings and as a boy I used to trace my fingers round the intricate patterns, but now it was rotting and home to all the creepy crawlies that you could imagine.

I stepped into the enormous hallway. It was just as I remembered. The elegant stairway that rose up and at the top went to the left and right. OOH it was good sliding down them. I remember that sometimes I was allowed to sit at the top and watch the people arrive, much excitement on their faces. I watched until I was gently taken very sleepily to my bedroom. Mum settled me with my favourite story.

But all this was a distant memory as I continued my tour of the house. My old playroom came next. I remember the beautiful rocking horse made by my dear father. It was grey and had a real leather saddle and reins, and a proper mane and tail. I used to gallop for miles on him till I was out of breath. Father used to draw pictures of horses for me to colour in. I had names for every one of them.

Then there were the times I helped mum in the kitchen on baking day there was always more stuff in my hair and in my mouth, than in the bowl. I did try and it always made my mother laugh. I loved my parents so much. I wish I could tell them right this minute. I can still see them but can't touch them and I don't understand why.

We used to go on picnics in the woods where fruit trees were in abundance and it was on these occasions that I learned so much about the animals and flowers that made the wood their home.

There was an old boat house down by the large lake and Dad used to take me fishing. Well, he would do the fishing and I would dangle my feet or my hands in the cool clear water. 'Be careful the fish don't bite,' Dad would say. I chuckled to myself when I remember the wonderful adventures we used to have. I kept pestering Dad to let me take the boat out on my own. After all I knew what to do, I had watched him often enough.

'I know about safety,' I used to plead, and he still kept telling me I wasn't big enough or strong enough. 'Hah,' I replied. 'I am very strong, I'm seven years old, look at my muscles. Dad always laughed when I did that, but he still refused to let me go out in the boat alone. One day, I'll show him, I muttered to myself and so continued to dangle my hands in the water.

It was several weeks later that my chance came. Dad had to go away on business and I knew where he kept the key to the boat house. I took it one morning and hid it down my wellies before my mum saw me. It was very hard to walk with a key pressing into the sole of my foot and soon I told my mum I was going out to play. She did not mind as I was allowed into the woods on my own, so that was where I told her that I was going. I did feel a little guilty, telling a fib, but I was so excited at the thought of proving to my father that I was not as silly as he imagined.

When I was out of sight of the house, I promptly removed the key from my wellies and ran like the wind down to the boat house. I knew I was doing wrong but there was no stopping me now. I finally got the key into the lock and got the boat down the water's edge. I knew how to row as my dad had taught me, but was only ever allowed to row when he was with me. The oars were still in it and I managed to row to the middle of the lake, then I stopped. Oh, it was so peaceful out here. I leaned over the edge of the boat as I had done many times before and looked at my reflection, I was so happy. I saw a fish and leaned a little further to try and touch it and at that moment the boat tipped and I was sucked down into the deep dark depths of the lake only to be trapped in the weeds at the bottom, everything went black.

It was many months later, that I was with my mother in the local village shop, and we both overheard two elderly women in the corner, talking about a small boy who was drowned in the lake at the Mansion house, his restless soul haunting the place apparently wanting to make amends to his parents for disobeying them.

We went outside and I looked up at my mother, she was sobbing openly. I wanted to comfort her but couldn't as my hand went straight through her body. I began to understand now. It was then that I realised that 'I 'was that young boy who had drowned in the lake.

Somewhere There is a Rainbow
by Carol Campbell

Next time you feel alone and at a total loss
Look for the positive things in life
Look to yonder
For the luscious green-covered hills.

Look that bit further where the sky touches
Gently stroking and holding its hand
Look for the puffballs, the cotton wool floating in the sky.
Look for nature's beauty
The sprays of colour gently waving in the wind.

Always remember the good
The positive issues in life
Lock the door on all negativity
Leave it behind.

Look for the rainbow
The bridge
The pathway to heaven
The meeting point, where we meet our loved ones

The shower in vibrant colours
Its just like crossing the ocean
Into the next domain
But our pathway is here
For the present
With the rainbow sent from heaven

La Cucina
by Olga Tramontin

Sitting outside the pavement café; watching the town clock as the time creeps to 10am. Going inside, running upstairs to the ladies' room, washing her hands for the third time. Drying them, warming them, under the blower/dryer. Must not have clammy hands for a handshake.

Outside again, sipping latte, hands cupped around the pretty floral mug. Another swift glance at the clock; Mum used to say never be late for an appointment, for school, even for a date. Mum was wise, warm, funny, especially when she sang in her lovely cracked voice. She had held Mum's hand when she drifted off into the long sleep. Ten years ago now...

Time to go. She hopes the metal chair hasn't impressed upon her skirt; straightens herself physically, mentally pats herself into shape. Here goes: he told her to be there at ten sharp; he rolled his 'r'.

'Don't be late,' he said. 'Because I haf to do my ordering at ten-thirty. And don't be early either,' he laughed. 'Because I haf to come down the stairs to let you in.'

She walks along the road, past a pub and, next to it, a guesthouse. It has an old bicycle wheel above the door with a sign saying 'Rest for the Tyred'. Opposite are several book shops and a solicitor's office. She thinks it was once famous for something, a murder?. She sees cars

65

turning into a petrol station. He has told her his *ristorante* is just before a petrol garage. Must be the one.

She arrives at the restaurant door, just as the town clock begins to strike ten.

Ellie thought he looked like Antonio Carluccio without the white hair. His was almost black with a few grey flecks in it, 'salt and pepper' hair came to mind. Yes, very apt – and to go with the dark curly hair were warm brown eyes, a generous mouth, all above a fat stomach encased in gleaming chefs' whites and blue-checked trousers. She wondered who did his laundry.

He shook her hand and called her Signorina Farfalla.

'My name's Ellie Summers,' she corrected him.

'Yeah, but you wear the farfalla in your hair, the butterfly.'

She touched it self-consciously and grinned. There was no hurry to take her other hand away from his warm one.

'My name is Bruno Longeretti, owner of La Cucina Ristorante. Please,' he added. 'Come and sit down. He led her to the far end of the restaurant; past tables with serviettes folded like little hats. Will I have to do them like that, she wondered.

Above them were balloon like lamps in rainbow colours, swaying with the breeze from the ceiling fan. Copper pots and pans hung on the whitewashed, rough-stone walls, interspersed with still-life paintings of food and wine.

La Cucina, he explained, was open plan. The restaurant being separated from the kitchen area, by a large, illuminated glass counter, inside which stood bottles of rosé wine, white wine and Peroni beer. There were stainless steel bowls, empty at the moment, but he told her they would later contain salads and fruit, maybe some delicious Italian dessert like Tiramisu.

Also hanging from the ceiling, immediately above the counter were several wine bottles encased in straw flasks, and various puppets, including one of a chef holding a wooden spoon (he looked like Signor Longeretti) and another of Pinocchio. Behind all these were large pieces of equipment, a huge oven and stove, a steel work table with a giant-sized chopping block, shelving that held pots of wooden spoons and over-sized kitchen tools made for big hands.

The pots and pans on more shelving made her tiny domestic pieces look like children's playthings. Below them a large, slotted block held at least a dozen assorted knives and beside it hung a gruesome cleaver. Ellie shuddered inwardly. She hoped the animals were dead when they were on the cutting edge of it.

There was a woman behind the counter, dressed in a red, white and green tabard.

'Hey Vicki,' he called her. 'Come and meet Signorina Ellie, la Farfalla.'

Perhaps Vicki was his wife?

'Vicki is my number one lady,' he said. 'She keeps the ristorante spotless and does all the washing up at night. She also puts up with my flying tempers,' he laughed.

Vicki gave a shy smile, displaying a need for a good dentist, and continued mopping the kitchen floor. Everything was shining, the huge amount of stainless steel and the floor to ceiling tiles behind the kitchen. In the restaurant itself, Ellie could smell polish and thought the dark brown tables looked immaculate. Good for Vicki. She glanced around the room, into the corners and on each wall, marvelling at the large and small items that embellished the restaurant. An Italianate Aladdin's cave.

'Hey Vicki, can you make us two coffees pliz my darling? Espresso for me… and for you, signorina?'

'Cappuccino please.'

'And a cappuccino for the young lady. And you, my darling, a cup of tea? Vicki doesn't like our Italian coffee,' he said to Ellie, 'she likes her tea.'

They sat down facing each other, Bruno with his large, sausage-fingered hands flat on the table. 'So, young lady, can you count? We don't have one of those clever tills here that tells you how much change to give.'

She nodded. 'Yes, I passed my GCSE's in Maths, English Lit., Geography, French and Home Economics. Oh, and Biology.'

He looked impressed. 'So, you can read and write, add up, and speak a foreign language. Plus cook and cut up frogs.' He pressed his lips together. 'Bene, good. Now, let me see your hands.'

Ellie looked at him in surprise. 'Pardon?'

'Your hands, hold them out, like this.' He held out his own in front of him, palm side down then palm side up.

Mystified, she complied.

'Multo bene, excellent. Beautiful clean nails and nicely manicured. I cannot,' he explained, 'employ someone, anyone, who has grubby hands or bites their nails. You wouldn't want to be served by someone like that, eh?'

'Erm, no.'

'Well Signorina Farfalla, you have the job. When can you start?'

Life's Changes
by Rosemarie David

Sunlight filtering through the blinds gave the room a golden glow, the only sound a rhythmic whoosh. Gillian sat looking at the faded posy clutched in her hand. The plump rose buds had lost their pink colour, the lacy collar was yellowed with age and the once pink and ivory ribbons were now a bleached calico. As she touched the dry petals of the flowers Gillian recalled the day that she had carried them with such hope. Her ivory lace gown and delicate veil clothed a young excited bride. It had been the happiest day of her life.

John had looked very smart in his dark suit with the stiff white collar and a carnation in his buttonhole. As he had slid the gold ring onto her finger her heart had swelled with pride.

Gillian had known John since she wore pig tails and bobby sox. Their carefree friendship had grown through the years from a wild passion into a deep, mature, comfortable warmth. When their son Michael was born they were overjoyed. He grew from a chubby toddler with tousled curls to a gangly youth always in the wars. He was their pride and joy and as he stood beside her chair now, he was his father's son, handsome, assured, a respected lawyer and a loving son.

The family had known difficult times through the years when money was short but they had weathered the storms together. She remembered days at the seaside, the fine sand that got into everything, ice creams that dripped sweet stickiness down their fingers. What fun it had all been. How quickly the time had slipped away, almost unnoticed.

No one should have to make the decision that she had had to make today. A slight pressure on her arm stirred Gillian from her revere and she rose from the chair. Gently she took her husband's hand in her free one, the other still clutching the posy. Leaning forward she whispered into his ear, then gently brushed her lips across his cheek. She was sure that she felt his hand tighten briefly around hers. A tear escaped and slid down her cheek followed by another.

Gillian let out a harsh sob and collapsed back into the chair still clutching John's hand in hers. She did not see Michael give a faint nod across the bed. There was a click and the room fell silent. With tears raining down his face Michael put his arm around his mother's heaving shoulders and, unnoticed by either of them, the man in the white coat quietly left the room. Gillian and Michael were alone with John their beloved husband and Father for the final farewell.

Love Lost
by Sue Whiting

There, under the rock, was the key,
A forgotten item in a forgotten world
He dared to go in. Would this be a sin?
Behind her back? What harm would it do?
He adjusted his mack, wet from the rain,
The rain hiding his ever flowing tears.

Could he go in? Turn back the years?
He entered into the quiet realm,
A realm where once there was so much love.
It was empty, empty of life,
There was not much left
No sign ever of painful strife.

He pretended in his mind, turning back time
To see his boys happy at play
Before their lives were so cruelly turned
Upside down, and he turned away,
Away in the lost world.
A world without warmth and love.

But it was a love that never dies,
Regardless of all the hurt and lies.

He turned to leave, silent tears falling.
He took the key and replaced it under the rock,
That was his life past,
Maybe nothing was meant to last.

The Colour Wheel
by Liz Penn

Bette listened with interest when told that 'If you want to take up water colour painting seriously always try to buy the best quality paints and materials that you can afford. Also make sure the palette holds twelve colours and each colour has its own place, then you know exactly where each is.'

By this time Bette was getting a little anxious, and looking at her watch she desperately wanted to get the 13 30 train back to Wellington, as it was the through train. She gave an inward sigh: Robert the art teacher was still talking, 'Take your colour wheel home with you, look and learn from it. I will see you all next week and see how well you are adapting to its uses.'

Why on earth Robert took his classes at Gas Street in Brum she never understood, but possibly it was because he originally came from that area, and, as his classes were well attended, she had decided to stay on for as long as she could and improve her visions of becoming a great artist .

Hurriedly Bette packed her art bag. She didn't bother to wash her palette just shoved it into a polythene bag along with her used paint brushes, a quick 'goodbye,' jacket on and was off out the door in no time.

Bette hurried down New Street as fast as her legs would carry her. She turned into the railway station, and reached the escalator, all the time thinking, 'which platform which platform? I must check.'

71

It came as a bit of a shock when she realised that she had to get to platform 4B, right at the top end. Down the steps she went only to see the back end of the 13.30 train pulling smoothly away out of the station. Disappointed, she looked around and luckily, spotting a uniformed porter, asked 'When is the next one please?' as by now she felt pretty exhausted.

'Fifteen minutes luv, there'll be one at 1 45' came the answer.'

Bette had no alternative but to sit down on one of those metal structures installed for use as seats just to patiently wait for the next connection.

Patience wasn't her best asset so she took out of her bag the picture of the colour wheel, which she had drawn and painted that morning, yellow and purple, blue and orange red and green. Not sure now what Robert the teacher meant, she thought awhile then put the picture away.

Fifteen minutes later she was on the train and, oh dear, it was stopping at Sandwell, Wolverhampton, Bilbrook, Codsall, Allbrighton, Cosford, Shifnal, and Telford,.the slower one she had wanted to avoid. Bette was in for a time-consuming ride to reach Wellington today,

Once again she took out her colour wheel to study the colours, 'Purple, yellow, orange and blue'. Her thoughts were broken by a voice saying, 'you like blue my dear.'

It was then she realised she had been speaking out loud, and turning to the elderly gentleman she happened to be sitting by, she answered him that yes she did like the colour blue. The gentleman then lifted his head and started to talk. 'I take very kindly to the blue of the Mediterranean plus all vibrant colours that you don't see in the U K. However I enjoy this train journey, because when we leave Wolverhampton we start to see the brightness of the fields, green and golden as we pass along from one station to another, and they just seem to glow.'

Bette forgot all about her colour wheel and was entranced by these lovely colours of nature as they passed by. All too soon the train arrived in Telford, and as the man shuffled to his feet he finally said, 'In Britain I find that colours are made more subtle and indeed this is their beauty.' He stretched himself slowly and departed with a 'This is my stop now.'

It was as Bette said her goodbyes that she saw the white stick he carried by his side and tapped his way expertly along and out of the carriage into the sunlight.

The Rose
by Carol Campbell

A rose was sent from a spirit
To bloom on earth for a short while
It grew in all its glory
And radiated love for all to see
In all directions of the compass
For everyone to see
It grew tall
It grew in strength
For everyone who saw it
The colour never faded
No matter what the weather
Its light always shone
Until one day it was time to return home
And bloom again
In the other world
Leaving a lasting memory
To live on in the hearts and minds
Of everyone who saw the beauty
Of the everlasting rose.

Our War 1939-1945
by Phyl Furniss

She was sitting at the piano, her fingers lightly touching the keys: not really playing anything, a pensive look on her face. He had just read from the daily newspaper that war was looming. As he sat at the table he stared across at her, then he spoke.

'We will have to think about the future. I don't want you to live in here, in London, it wouldn't be safe.'

'Andrew darling,' she said quietly. Will this mean we will be separated? I don't think I could bear that.'

Andrew stood up and went over to his wife, took her hands in his. 'Mary darling,' he murmured. She stood up, put her arms round his neck and he kissed her gently on the forehead. 'You know I'd hate to be separated from you, but I would feel happier if I knew you were somewhere safe.'

'Yes, that too will have to be sorted out.' He folded the paper neatly and placed it on the table in front of him. Dad was a neat and tidy man, methodical.

'What about Lucy?' she asked.

At that moment I burst through the door. I am Lucy, their only child. I was fourteen then, and went to a private college for young ladies. I had been out for the day with friends. We'd been to the stables and I had ridden a beautiful chestnut horse through the countryside of Surrey.

'I've had a wonderful day.' I said, and proceeded to rattle on about the amazing I had had. 'I wish it could go on forever, but' I continued. 'The new term starts next week, so it'll be ages before I can go again. Mummy, you look upset. Is anything wrong?' I asked, realising I'd been talking so much I hadn't noticed that both my parents had a look of gloom. They were normally such a happy couple, always laughing and teasing each other.

'We've been thinking about the future sweetheart,' said my father. 'If this war starts it will mean changes for us all.'

'Oh Daddy, I haven't given it a thought. Do you really think there will be war?'

'Yes Lucy, I do. And we must all be brave and do what is best, even though we might not like it.'

During the next two months my father spent time finding a suitable home for my mother and I to live in. Fortunately, Daddy knew an estate agent who had country properties on his books, and was able to purchase a modest cottage. It had a small garden and was quite near a farm. Although it was small it struck me as quaint and I felt quite at home there.

At first we only used the cottage at weekends. I went back to college until something else could be decided about my future. On 3rd September 1939, Neville Chamberlain announced to the nation that we were at war

It was a Sunday morning, about 11am. We were all in church and the vicar suggested we went home. From that day onwards, life was never the same.

I went away to boarding school to finish my education and Mummy lived in her cottage in the country. Daddy worked at the War Office in London. We all longed for the rare times we could be together, usually at the cottage.

Mummy did her best to be brave. She went to work at the nearby farm and, surprisingly, quite enjoyed it. We both worried about Daddy staying in London, prayed his office didn't get bombed.

As for me, I stayed at boarding school until war ended in 1945, when our lives changed again... but that's another story.

That's Youth
by Louise McClean

I study my grandson as he lolls over a chair in the lounge. He's giving his attention to a Gameboy which his fingers flutter over constantly. His legs go on for ever and his feet and hands seem to be enormous. When did he get so tall and change from a cute, cuddly little boy to this monosyllabic gangling stranger?

So, ok, we'll have a go at conversation.

Me: "How's things at college, Peter?"

Peter (never lifting his eyes from the Gameboy)   "OK"

Me: "Do you get much homework this year?"

Peter (still not looking up)   "Too much"

Me: "Did you get the money I sent you for your birthday last month?"

Peter (still playing with the damned Gameboy)   "Oh yeh, thanks"

I almost give up but decide to plod on.

Me: "Have you got a girlfriend yet?"

Peter (blushing slightly, I notice)   "Don't be silly Gran"

I study him more closely and I can well believe that last answer because, quite honestly, who else except his mother and me would want him at the moment? His hair, which used to curl so cutely, is now greasy and plastered thick, with some sort of gel, and it sticks up in spikes all over his head.

His skin looks dull and unhealthy, and if he isn't shaving yet he should be. Though, in fairness, it would be difficult with all those spots on his face. Maybe I should tell him about that cream which is good for spots: then again, maybe not.

He's wearing a huge, loose, creased black-and-grey top with a hideous, garish design on the front. His jeans hang off his skinny hip bones and seem to get wider as they go down, so that they flap over his filthy trainers and trail along the ground.

My daughter, his mother, comes in with a mug of coffee and sets it down beside him. He ignores her totally and fiddles on with the Gameboy. I bristle, but decide to say nothing: it's not my place to do so really.

Mother: "It might be an idea to tidy your bedroom. I can't tell the clean clothes from the dirty ones lying all over the floor."

Peter (sighing loudly) "Oh God! There's no peace in this house. It's nag, nag, nag from morning till night. I'm sick of it. I'm going out."

And off he goes, accidentally kicking over the coffee as he passes.

I look at his mother and start to say, "In my day…" but then I stop because it's not my day now, it's his day. I had my day and did it my way, and now it's his turn and he is living his, his way.

I know, in my heart, that this is just a stage he's going through and, hopefully, in another few years I will have my lovely, loving grandson back.

So I shut up and smile at my daughter as she begins to mop up the coffee.

Night Noises
by Rosemarie David

I thought I heard a noise. What could it be? I sat up in my bed and listened. Yes, there it was again. A faint scratching. Could it be Tabby, the neighbour's cat, wanting to come in from the cold night air?

My neighbour was away and I was looking after her cat. Cats, what a nuisance they could be at times. I threw back my duvet and getting out of bed I snuggled my feet into thick sheepskin slippers. All was still and then it came again. A faint scratching. I walked through the dark house, listening intently as I moved slowly towards the sound. Then I heard another sound, a cat meowing outside my back door. Turning the key I opened the door and called "Here kitty come in Tabby".

The policeman surveyed the tragic scene in front of him: the open door, the ransacked house and the elderly lady on the floor. Her eyes open and staring, her mouth a gaping scream. The knife still protruded from her chest and blood had pooled around her. Not another one, he thought to himself. This killer was clever and preyed on the vulnerable. He knew most folk kept a cat. Poor soul's – they fell for it every time.

Then he saw it. The notice that had been pushed through letter boxes just the day before by his colleague. It read, in large letters:

> DO NOT OPEN YOUR DOOR WITHOUT USING
> YOUR DOOR CHAIN, CHECKING THROUGH A
> WINDOW, OR ASKING WHO IT IS.
> THERE IS A DANGEROUS CRIMINAL AT LARGE
> WHO SCRATCHES AT THE DOOR AND MEOWS,
> PRETENDING TO BE A CAT ASKING TO BE LET IN.
> DO NOT TAKE A CHANCE.

Then he looked at her face again. His heart sank: her eyes were white and cloudy. Mavis had not read the notice: she could not – she was blind.

Strange Encounter on a Train
by Carol Campbell

Ruth rushed along the platform to board her train. Her weekend bag packed, she was going on a well-deserved long weekend, travelling back up to Edinburgh to visit her childhood friend. They had remained close by letter and phone for thirty something years, but now there was going to be a well-deserved party for these two friends to truly to catch up,

Ruth had recently split with James: it had been a whirlwind romance, getting married within weeks of meeting (at forty two she hadn't wanted to be left on the shelf), but after a disastrous couple of weeks they both decided to go their separate ways.

As Ruth took her seat, she took her diary from her bag and started to write: 12.12.2012

'Well I'm finally going to visit Samantha to catch up on the good old days, a well needed break, time to let my hair down methinks.'
She could suddenly smell pipe tobacco and lifted her eyes to see where it was coming from, but no one was there, The next sound she heard was the conductor saying 'tickets please'.

For a moment she was back in reality, listening to the whooshing of the wind as the train travelled through it at full pelt, almost like a bullet being fired from a gun, but this was a difference it was a fast moving express train, riding back to the good old days.

She took her ticket from her purse and smiled and looked back down at her diary to continue her entry, just then everything seemed to go dark, as the train entered a tunnel full speed ahead. She blinked as her entry read 12.12.1919. Then she looked down at her dusty coloured ankle length skirt and brushed out creases to neaten her lap. She sighed deeply as the journey had been long and tiring. She could smell the coal in the air even taste it in the back of her throat. The train wheels spoke repeatedly almost like the chorus of a song, the sound chasing around in her mind as she looked at her entry in her diary. She was gazing down at a tear-stained page. It spoke about her beloved James, her undying love for him and her loss, as he had died too, and how she could never ever love anyone again, the pain was too great and here she was an unmarried mother-to-be being sent away, far away, her family didn't want the disgrace being put upon their name, after all they were outstanding pillars of the community: what would their parishioners say?

Catherine was meant to be a child of the cloth, and now her future husband was gone, she had never felt so alone, but she was. As the train approached the end of the tunnel the lights seemed to dim as it emerged into daylight. Soon it approached yet another station. Not long now Ruth thought and the adventure will begin. Just then a gentleman sat opposite her she couldn't help but notice his gaze, he had the most brilliant blue eyes she had ever seen. She smiled faintly as he asked, 'Is your book good?

She giggled and said, 'Hope so, I'm just logging my diary.'

'I'm William,' said the dashing hunk sitting across from her.

She smiled. 'I'm Ruth. I'm going home to an old friend's reunion.'

'That's strange I'm going back home for a school reunion too.' His voice was so soft, her heart almost skipped a beat. She'd not felt this way since being a teenager.

William said, 'This is a coincidence we're both travelling back for reunions, don't you think? Do you believe in coincidences?

Ruth laughed, as the train passed through yet another tunnel.

Catherine looked up, 'James,' she said. And his blue-eyed gaze caught hers. A tear trickled down her cheeks.

James smiled, 'Catherine I told you I would never leave you and I would travel through time to find you. When I said I loved you I meant it would be forever.'

As the train came to a halt William smiled at Ruth and said, ' Thank you for your company. Can I see you again?'

Ruth giggled like a silly young teenager. 'I would love to,' she said. This was definitely the start of a new entry in her diary.

The New Spring Day
by Phyl Furniss

A warm sun rises from its bed
Greeting the day that lies ahead
Creating bright colour and warm glow
Over the landscape far below.

The song of the birds as they wake at dawn
They fly from their nests and search for food
A juicy fat worm appears on a lawn
Breakfast for one of their brood.

Spring has arrived like a new lease of life
Trees bursting into bud wake from winter sleep
Grass grows from its roots, new greenness appears
Noise from the mower fills the new season air

Daisies fly up through the blade cuts like fairies
Dancing along with the gold buttercups
Awake too are creatures from their long hibernation
Searching for food is their intention.

Ducks swim on the pond, fowl scratch on the farm
Sheep in the meadow with lambs skitting around
People in streets all bustling and busy
Life is awake there is so much sound.

Buses, lorries, cars, bicycles too
The noise of a train with a tunnel to go through
A long day ahead, with plenty to do
Till the day turns to night and darkness falls.

Everywhere quiet, soon sleep will descend
And so the new day has come to an end.

Ralph!
by Maureen Thomas

The newspaper headline stared straight back at me! It said, 'HAVE YOU SEEN THIS MAN? *His name is Ralph, and he needs urgent medical attention.*" There was a picture of a rather dishevelled man with a beard, moustache and long, lank hair.

'How could anyone recognise HIM,' I thought? But this article intrigued me and I went into the newsagent's and bought the paper which contained the article, walked to the park and sat on a bench to read about this unfortunate man.

He was fortyish, suffering from type one diabetes, and had apparently been found in a crumpled heap in a doorway a few days earlier. The person who had discovered him had fortunately realised that he wasn't just asleep, he was in a coma, and had called an ambulance. This prompt action had saved Ralph's life. The article went on to plead for his family to come forward.

I was sad at the thought of his family, desperately looking for him, and what could happen if he did not receive the treatment he needed. Ralph had apparently discharged himself before receiving his medicines.

I then thought about my own father. He left Mum and me when I was just seven years old. He just went to work one day and never returned. Everything was done to try and find him, but it did no good: now, he was just a vague memory. It hurt, and I missed him so much, but Mum flatly refused to talk about him.

All she said was ' Becky, as far as I'm concerned he is dead.' I was horrified, because I wanted to know more about my father and the reason why he left. I had no photograph to treasure, just vague memories of days out, or walks in the very park where I was now sitting. I was 20 years old now and Mum had shut my dad out of our lives as though he had never existed.

It was this article that made me want to go home and do something to help. He must have family somewhere. When I got home, Mum was in the kitchen and I gave her the newspaper. She read the article, then sat down and stared at the picture. I could see that it affected her in such a way that she just ran from the room.

A few days later, I found her in her bedroom looking at a framed photograph. A single tear rolled down her cheek, her finger rested on the glass. I quietly went in and saw that it was a picture of a very handsome man with deep brown eyes and dimples. She said it was my father. I didn't realise that she had kept this picture: it came as a complete surprise.

We hugged and cried together and Mum then explained that she didn't want to give me false hope that my dad would ever come back and all these years had hidden from me the only memory she had of him. It was the article in the paper that had made her realise how very selfish she had been, not talking to me about my father.

A few days passed and I still could not get Ralph out of my mind. The article had said how he had recently been seen shuffling his way round the streets and the park, and was regarded as the kind of beggar you would see in most towns. Then he was found by a Good Samaritan and had been taken to hospital.

Another headline appeared in the local paper a few days later 'DO YOU KNOW THIS MAN?' I knew him alright. It was Ralph. He was found, and had been reluctantly taken to hospital and was now receiving his proper treatment, but the police were still trying to find his family.

I decided to go to the hospital to see if I could talk to him and to hopefully try to get him a happy ending. The nurses said he was a most sad and unusual case as this man did not say anything about himself, except that his name was Ralph. He told them he was very sorry and was seeking forgiveness for something he had done many years before.

I gingerly entered his room with one of the nurses and walked slowly to his bed; he seemed to be asleep. At least he was now clean shaven and had had his long hair cut to make him look presentable. He opened his eyes and it was then that I saw the man in the photograph that Mum had kept for so many years.

His brown eyes that lit up when he saw me and the dimples showed when he smiled and said, 'Becky, is it really you? Can you ever forgive me?'

We hugged so tightly and cried rivers. The lost years just slipped away, just like my dad did. Now I held him in my arms.

Such is Life
by Carol Campbell

Life is an adventure
Full of twists and turns
As we grow
Each day we learn
As a baby we learn to talk
We learn to walk
As we walk we will stumble and fall
But in life's twists and turns we will learn to get back up again

---

Ghost Riders in the Sky
by Rosemarie David

Jim was only 17 and it was his first cattle drive so he was often teased and picked on by the seasoned riders. They constantly played pranks on him and he tried not to let them see how nervous he was but tonight was different. He was riding the midnight watch and as the storm clouds raced across the skies he was not sure that he could keep his horse calm when he felt so on edge. Singing softly to the cattle he held his reins loosely as his horse ambled amongst them. The only sounds were the gentle creak from his saddle leather and the muffled moans from the restless animals as the wind picked up.

Around the fire earlier in the evening, while eating bean stew and drinking black coffee, Jim had been told the story of the ghost riders chasing the devils herd that raced across the dark stormy skies – just like the one overhead tonight. They told him to be alert to anything unusual but not to scare the cattle as a stampede would be disastrous. Jim was sure that they were just trying to scare him and laughed at them but inside he shook like a bowl of jello.

Then Jim thought he heard a soft whistle from the nearby bushes and his horse stopped and pricked his ears towards the sound. Placing his gloved hand on the trembling neck he tried to soothe the mustang. The cattle started to shuffle restlessly and Jim looked around him. He could not see much in the darkness except for the bulky shapes of the animals. He called out softly to his fellow outrider but there was no reply. Gathering his reins Jim turned his horse and began to make his way slowly around the herd and towards the camp.

Then it happened. A sudden gust of wind was followed by a deep rumble and a flash lit the night sky. His horse and the cattle reacted as one. Was the bellowing from the animals around him or the sky above? Jim had no time to think as he was almost unseated by his horse. As the mad dash began he was caught in the middle of the frenzy. Fear shot through him like a thunderbolt. He had to remain in the saddle or he would be trampled by the crazed herd. All he could hear was the wind and the bellowing of cattle as his horse raced on. Suddenly his horse stumbled and fell beneath the thundering iron hooves, taking Jim with him into the flood of heaving bodies.

'How strange,' Jim thought as he sat on his horse looking down upon the calmly grazing herd of longhorns. He was sure he was riding outpost tonight but he did not seem to belong somehow. He pulled on the leather reins and saw fire coming from his horse's nostrils. It was then that Jim realised that he was one of those ghost riders in the sky, and sadness filled him when he realised that he would never again feel the prairie wind in his face and smell the dust from the trail. He thought he heard someone call his name and looked around.

'Jim.' The voice was louder this time and then he felt a rough shake of his arm.

'Wake up, Jim. It's time for your midnight watch.'

Flood
by Olga Tramontin

It was weird, this eerie silence; no wind to ripple the waters, no birdsong from the blackened, leafless trees. Nothing. No humanity save for me. The only sound came from the gentle lapping of my oars as I rowed softly, fearfully, through these murky waters towards what must be land. It was barely visible through the mist, a few clumps of what might be grassy banks; the odd tree looming within that strange light, broken, naked of nature's clothing, like a crippled beggar.

I was so intent on piercing the gloom I almost rowed into a small tree that appeared in the muddied waters, its few visible branches looking frighteningly like sharks' fins. Quickly I righted my flimsy kayak, guided it beyond the tree. Did that mean I was rowing over land that was flooded, or the river itself? Was the tree still rooted or had it been torn from its true resting place and was now caught in underwater detritus that had made its way down from the mountain to flooded valley and swift flowing river?

It seemed I had been rowing for hours, days, weeks, through relentless rain and terrifying storms. Where only lightning lit up the sky and down onto this punished land. I don't remember sleeping, or being aware when night became this sepia, misty day, that showed off its graveyard of broken trees and barren distant land over there. I steered the kayak towards those far off edifices, praying a silent prayer for a sound other than my paddles as they skimmed the water either side of me. It was human sound I desired. Someone, anyone calling out, 'Hey there. Over here. Come ashore.'

Or the flapping of a water bird's wings, the croak of a frog, the caw of a crow that had found food on outlying fields beyond my vision. Was it too much to ask? Could I really be the only one left in this desolate, soaked land?

There was a sound, not flapping wings or croaking or from a distant crow. More like the wind rustling among unseen trees. I stopped rowing, listened, watched with a frightened fascination as the mist suddenly cleared before me. A watery sun appeared, so clothed in the mist I could stare at it without hurting my eyes, note its perfect circle, a disc millions of miles away but visible after days and weeks of its hiding from the earth.

A breeze got up and bullied my small craft towards the shore that, only moments before, I had glimpsed through that yellowy haze. Seconds later the kayak bumped into something so solid I was almost jolted overboard. Not grassy bank or reeds, but a broken wooden farm gate, its rusted hinges hanging onto one of the uprights of its frame.

Perhaps, I thought, the waters I have floated upon for indeterminate time are not river or floating lake, but flooded land? Somewhat awkwardly I climbed out, scrambled over the broken farm gate and stepped onto muddied grass. I grabbed my small backpack, light now and empty of food and most of the bottle of stale water that had made up my meagre survival diet.

The mist cleared for a hundred, maybe two hundred metres, enabling me to see the devastation caused by the storms. Fences down, great, hundred year old oaks reduced to jagged trunks, their branches scattered over fields that once were lush with corn and barley.

Still no sound, except for the wind and my laboured breathing. It was difficult to walk on the mud-soaked land, mournful to witness the desolation. There was no sign of any buildings, no farmhouse, barns or machinery, no tractor or ploughing tools. Nothing. No-one, not a single human being or animal. No sheep, cattle, goats or horses, not even a wild rabbit. Surely, I thought, that farm gate back there meant there must have been a farm here?

I stumbled forward, rapidly losing hope but nevertheless going away from the river and floods. As I moved onwards so the mist before me cleared a little more, revealing other broken trees, fences, and barren earth. I came upon it, looked at it, weirdly unaware for a moment of its inappropriateness in that place. I stared then, in disbelief. How could it be? What caused it to survive when everything around it had been so totally destroyed?

A tree, but not just any tree. An apple tree bent under the weight of its own fruit, ready for picking. My mouth watered. I hadn't eaten for several days, except for a soaked biscuit that had hidden in the bottom of my backpack.

Cautiously I walked towards it, my eyes darting to right and left as if I expected an angry farmer to chase me. No-one came. I picked an apple from a lower branch, twisting it as I had been taught until it came off easily.

I took a bite, a small one at first until I was sure that it was real fruit and not something of my imagination. Yes, it was real, with a sweetness that I had never tasted before. I took another bite, larger than the tentative first one, crunching its sweetness between my eager teeth.

Hunger overcame curiosity as to why this tree had survived. But three apples on and I began to feel discomfort. My stomach protested and my throat hurt after swallowing such solid food. Seconds later I vomited up all I had eaten, leaving a white and green mess on the ground.

Maybe the tree was bewitched, placed there to lure the unwary? Perhaps the fruit was poisoned? How, and by whom? Surely my imagination was playing tricks? Maybe the tree only existed in my demented mind? The mess at my feet was real enough and, not only could I see the apple tree, I could touch it, handle its fruit and smell them.

A great tiredness swept over me. The sun was disappearing again within the mist. Once more the land put on a sepia cloak with the odd blackened tree piercing its gloom. The air around me was moist with droplets that fell from my hair onto the damp clothes I was dressed in.

'Please, no more floods,' I prayed. The apple tree had gone. Where? When? The damp earth held only broken bits of tree and fence and scarce remains of what had once been fields of corn and barley. I stumbled back towards the river, hoping my kayak would be there intact, but it was not where I left it.

Panic set in. In this torment around me I knew I could not take anymore. My mind was as broken as the land.

I heard a whimpering sound, like a small puppy crying for its mother. The sound came from within my head, out of my mouth. It was me who was whimpering. I shut my eyes wanting to shut out the horror about me. Then I felt a warmth, a comforting feeling of rescue and safety.

'Hush darling,' said my man. 'It's only a dream. You're having a bad dream. I'm here... Love you.'

I turned over, still wrapped in his arms, and I slept.

Toasted Teacakes and a Colonoscopy
by Sue Whiting

Jane almost stumbled through the door under the weight of shopping she carried. She looked round for an empty table but couldn't see one. Not until she spotted Gladys. She weaved her way towards her.

'Oh Jane, you look shattered. Come and take the weight off for a bit. It's good to see you.'

Jane almost fell into the chair with exhaustion. 'Gladys! Fancy seeing you here. Are you well?'

'Actually Jane, I've had a few problems. In fact I went to the doctor's this morning.'

She leaned forward and looked around her before adding in a whisper, 'It's me waterworks, they're not right you know. I told the doctor, in fact I went with a list, told him what I thought was wrong, cos I looked it up on the internet.'

'Fancy you getting it up on the 'net,' said Jane all ears.

'Yes, the doctor wasn't best pleased though, but as I said, I wanted to save him time.'

'I'll have toasted teacake and a pot of tea thank you,' said Jane when the waitress came to their table.

'I told the doctor what I thought was wrong, but he didn't seem to take any notice. Which I thought was quite rude after all my trouble looking it up,' said Gladys, who by this time was on her second cup of tea.

'So what did the doctor say it was then?' asked Jane, wishing the waitress would hurry up as she was gasping.

'Well, he didn't actually say what it was at all.' Gladys leaned forward again in the whisper mode. 'He wants me to take a sample... you know.'

Jane laughed. 'He wants you to pee in one of those little bottles. It's so hard to do,' she added, happy the waitress had arrived with her order.

'That's it, Jane, I've got to wee in the bottle and take it to the surgery.'

Jane poured herself a cup of tea and then started to butter her teacake, which was lovely and warm. 'At least they'll know what's wrong with you then.' She mumbled over a mouthful of teacake. 'What did you think was wrong?'

'I think it's cystitis, you know... a wee infection.'

Jane tried not to contemplate this whilst she was eating. Gladys continued, 'I've got to wait for the test results before he will even think of giving me anything for it.' She leant forward again. 'It really stings you know,' she mouthed to Jane.

'I know it does dear, I've had it myself. Real nasty it is,' Jane said as she poured herself a second cup of tea. She wished she had another teacake because she was still quite hungry. She hadn't eaten since yesterday because of her hospital appointment. But now that was over and done with she felt quite starved. 'I've just come from the hospital myself,' she said, putting sugar in her cup. 'So glad it's over with.'

'So glad what's over with?' inquired Gladys, getting a tissue out of her handbag.

'Well I suppose I can tell you now that I've finished eating.' Jane shuffled forward on her seat and bent her head towards her friend. 'I've been for a colonoscopy.'

Gladys looked decidedly shocked. 'You never have,' she gasped. 'Not one of them tests where they put a camera up... you know...'

'Yes, one of them, and it wasn't pleasant I can tell you. I had to have all these laxatives the night before and boy, did they give me some gip.' Jane finished her tea, then continued. 'Yes, you get to see your insides on this telly thing. It's disgusting.'

'Oh my lord,' said Gladys. 'I bet it is. You poor thing.'

'Well it's done now,' said Jane. 'Just got to wait for the results.'

'What do you think it is then?' Gladys asked as she rooted round in her bag for her purse.

'Don't know really. Anyway it's probably nothing. As I told my George, only the good die young, so I shall live forever,' she said with a giggle.

'How is old George?' she asked, still rooting around for her purse.

'Oh, you know, his arthritis is giving him gip and his gout is playing up, but otherwise he's ok.'

Jane stood up to put her coat on. 'Anyway, Gladys, it was great bumping into you like this.' She did her top button up and reached for her scarf. 'I hope your test results are ok.'

'Yours too,' said Gladys. 'We're a right pair aren't we?' She leant forward and gave Jane a peck on the cheek. They both made their way to the counter to pay.

'Well I expect we shall bump into each other again before long,' said Gladys as she walked out of the café. 'Give my love to George and take care won't you?'

'Yes, 'bye Gladys. See you again...'bye.' Jane waved as she walked down the road to catch her bus. So nice to catch up with old friends...

The House in the Outback
by Liz Penn

Mae heard the door go bang and smiled to herself as she thought that He hadn't asked her to get up and give him breakfast. She stepped out of the room they had slept in and went through to the parlour. The tin mug on the table was still warm so he had had a hot drink after all and she was delighted to see the Damper she had made yesterday had nearly all gone. She knew she should not have wasted the flour, but had wanted to try her hand with her limited resources at making something easy, and it had worked. When she had turned the loaf out of the wood stove oven it looked brown and wholesome, and today Ned had eaten nearly all of it for breakfast. Satisfied at this Mae put her hands on her swollen stomach, already the warmth of the morning was about to tell her it was going to be another hot and humid day.

Ned realised it was nearly her time, and everything was still strange to her, but if only he could find the gold everyone was digging for, things would change. He had been lucky and found one nugget already which he had taken to the local town of Ballaret, where the shady dealer had given him four pounds; which was wonderful. This had enabled him to purchase a cow, who now gave them enough milk to share at a cost to a few folks living beyond the hill.

Ned knew food was scarce, but he would dig today like mad until he found at least one more gold nugget, after all men had made fortunes in this year of 1850.

Mae washed her face and hands in the wooden pail used as a sink, she had to attend to the few vegetables growing outside where they had scattered the seeds they brought out from England and miraculously they had some potatoes and onions growing, which were good for soup and much better than that awful kangaroo meat Ned had bought home a few days ago. Mae had told him she would not cook or eat it, which Ned answered by saying that they lived in the outback, and they must eat as other people did in the outback.

Mae trudged down to the river, carrying her wooden pail; which was heavy even without the water, but this was a daily job that had to be done. She would collect the water and then intended going back to make that lining in her old wooden chest kept in the bedroom. She stooped to fill up the bucket and a pair of brown hands came towards her and took the heavy pail off her. It was Daisy, her Aborigine friend. Mae named her Daisy because she could not understand a word she said and always had small flowers in her hair.

Daisy was caring for Mae. She made the journey once a week from her settlement to attend to at least three other ladies in the area who were within weeks of each other to give birth. Mae was grateful and knew she was in good hands.

Slowly they walked back to the rough wooden house, and after both drinking some milk, Daisy examined Mae and nodded her head in approval. Smiling she then put on the table the wild berries she bought for all of her 'Moms to be', waving a Good-Bye she continued on her journey through the dust and heat of the day.

Mae cleared up the used utensils, checked outside to make sure their cow was safely chewing the grass outside, and retreated to their bedroom. She opened the chest and took out a lovely white gown and held it to her; it had a scalloped hem and lace bodice. She sighed, and thought it wouldn't fit her anyway, for a while.

Ned came home tired and hungry, no gold today, but was surprised to see the table laid out with bowls. Mae was there and she had cooked onion and potato soup again, plus delicious looking berries too, but not having eaten all day it was a rare feast for him.

Later when Ned had washed and rested a while Mae ushered him into the bedroom. He entered rather hesitantly, then he saw that their old chest had been turned into a thing of beauty, and was now a crib, lined with satin and lace. A label held on with white ribbon read, 'OUR BABY'; Ned took Mae in his arms, maybe a house in the outback wasn't that bad after all.

Sometimes
by Carol Campbell

Sometimes we need to accept who we are
To understand who we are
And why we have travelled so far on the path we are on
Which may or may not be the one we feel is right or wrong for us
Either way we got here
We travelled this far
And there's a reason why
To enable us to grow and learn
And to become strong
We are that even if we don't feel that way
Take it and believe it we are.

Just One Man
by Rosemarie David

Great Spirit, as my hair turns to silver and my eyes grow dim I think on the days of my youth. I feel again the warmth of my pony between my thighs and I hear the war cries around us as her hooves thunder across the plain. I feel the comfort of my woman beside me and see the strength of my growing son. I watch children playing in the dust and the camp dogs sleeping in the shade. I drink the fresh clear water of the mountain stream and I am at one with the earth.

My years have been many and both sorrows and joys were scattered in the path of my moccasins. I taste again the freshly roasted buffalo meat beside the campfire after a hunt and enjoy the shelter of my tepee on an icy winter's night. I reach down beside me and bury my fingers in the thick grey coat of my faithful dog who shares the winter of my days and I feel his breath.

Today I tell stories to the children of past glories and at last I begin to understand your way for my people. I do not know when you will call me to ride the gentle winds of Father Sky but I see at last that each life is a thread to brighten the design of the cloth you weave. All are important. It is your web of life which begins and ends with just one man.

Attingham Park
by Ruth Broster

As I lay here in the midday sun
The bees fly by
Sounding their delicate hum
Unperturbed I shall be
As I view the glory of you elegantly
Standing loud and proud
for all of us to see
Within a glisten you draw the crowd
And share your vanity.

The House in the Forest
by Olga Tramontin

It was my Grandfather's place, in the forest. I don't know its name. We only referred to it as the forest, and the house as Grandfather's house. It was a magical place in a little clearing, where rabbits played in the early morning sun and foxes barked in the still of the night.

It was stone built, with a thick oak door and window frames, a roof made of logs and felt to keep out winter storms and the spring rains. Downstairs was one huge room, with nooks and crannies that served as kitchen, dining area and a place to sit cosily around the huge wood stove, for warmth on chilly nights. There were two wooden settles made by Grandfather, with hand stitched cushions that Grandmother had made in her day. A handmade rug, also made by her, on the floor in front of the fire was where I liked to lay when Grandfather told me stories of when he was a boy. He sat in his rocker chair smoking his clay pipe and gazing into the open door of the wood stove, his eyes twinkling as they reflected the flames.

Grandmother had died before I was born and her photograph was set on the mantelshelf, along with his spare pipe and curious lighter. It resembled a metal tube with a wheel that you flicked with your thumb to produce the spark that ignited a petrol-soaked wick. I was eight before I could master the action and produce a flame. Grandfather smiled at me, patted my head and told me I was a good boy.

I used to stay in that house in the forest with Grandfather every summer while my parents went away to work I supposed. I was never specifically told where they went or what they did during those glorious months of summer. I did not really care. Staying with Grandfather was a magical interlude between two school terms.

Each morning we would go deeper into the forest and examine the traps that Grandfather had set the night before. Sometimes there would be a rabbit, occasionally a wild pheasant and often a long eared hare caught there. If I cried or complained, Grandfather would say, 'We only kill to eat. There are plenty that get away to live their lives.'

We collected wild berries, herbs and garlic to flavour the stews that he made. Delicious they were, with potatoes dug from a small plot near the house that he called his allotment, and crusty bread to dip in the gravy.

We walked into town every few days along the forest path that was too narrow for a car, barely wide enough for a pony and cart. Grandfather had neither. We enjoyed the walk, listening to birdsong or the bleating of sheep in adjoining fields to the forest. It was not far, maybe two miles there and two miles back. The town was not really a town; apart from a few houses and cottages it boasted three shops, an inn, a church and a hall where the people met once in a while to discuss important matters.

We would buy bread and butter, tea and coffee, sugar and a tin of powdered milk for when Grandfather's tethered goat failed to give milk. Grandfather grew his own vegetables in season and gathered the fruits of the forest. But he would buy me apples; large red ones that he rubbed on his jacket sleeve to make them shine. I was convinced they tasted better because he polished them so vigorously.

When our purchases were complete we would visit the inn, sit in a corner at a large round table with several other old men, all of whom Grandfather knew by name. They drank frothy beer out of pewter tankards, lick the froth from their beards and moustaches. I was given sparkling lemonade and a packet of crisps with a dark blue sachet of salt to sprinkle over them.

They would talk about the good old days, when they were young. Maybe play a few games of dominoes which they held in one hand like a fan of cards and banged them down onto the scrubbed wooden table matching the black spots on the white ivory until one of them was out of dominoes.

The winner bought another round of ale and a lemonade for me, if I had drained my glass. After three or four such games, we would gather our hessian bags and return to the house in the forest, Grandfather hiccupping on the way.

One summer he whittled a horse for me from one of the fallen trees beyond the house and its clearing. Another time he made me a little handcart that I could pull to the shops and carry our purchases home. He gave me one of his old knives and taught me how to carve simple things with it. Wisely he told me only to use the knife to create things, never as a weapon. Enough knives and guns had been used to destroy lives is what he said...

That was many years ago. I have children of my own now. The old man is long gone and my parents eventually moved abroad. Libby and I enjoy taking our children on summer holidays. We visit all kinds of places, but their favourite one is when we stay in the house in the forest that Grandfather left to me, his only grandson...

Lost Souls
by Maureen Thomas

She glides gracefully across the water, such a sad figure, swirling and swaying in the misty evening. She howls as she waits for her lost love, her hollow eyes searching for any sign of his return, she will not rest until she is in his arms again.

Meanwhile, at the old inn near the harbour's edge, it was business as usual. The local fishermen having moored their boats were having a long deserved rest before they went home. The old place was humming and welcoming.

Old Ned sat in the corner underneath a picture that depicted the loss of a crew of fishermen. It named the men concerned and it was put on the wall when they were lost at sea fifteen years previously doing the job they loved. One of the wives was so very depressed and mourned her husband so much that she jumped from the cliff into the sea to be with him, and she haunts the area every year since then.

Two strangers came into the inn, purchased their drinks and sat at the table in the corner with Ned .He didn't waste much time in starting up a conversation, telling the two men of his travels, and as they all sat by the large burning fire the two strangers were beginning to feel very comfortable and warm. They noticed that Ned had a very weather worn face, brown and cracked with age. A white beard covering his chin and a flat cap on his head, they also noticed that he could certainly down the rum!

As the evening progressed, one of the strangers looked up at the picture above Ned's head and asked him who the men were and what happened that fateful night. That was when they noticed a change in Ned, his blue eyes looked very distant as he told them the story of those poor men.

Everything had started out as normal that morning. Jack, Edward and Bill had been prepared to be away for a few days. They had had a really good first day of fishing but the second day nothing, so they had decided to go further away from their usual place, when the weather took a turn for the worse. A very strong wind began to rock their little boat and they started to experience a storm so fierce that they tried to radio for help but alas they all perished in the sea and never returned home. Their boat was never found and that night the village had lost three very brave men.

Ned had tears in his eyes as he told his story and one of the men went to the bar to get him yet another rum. His friend was warming his hands in front of the fire when he returned and asked where Ned had gone. They both looked at his seat, it was empty, and there was no way Ned could have got out without them both knowing.

They went to the bar and asked the landlord if they had seen him. They described him and told him his name and what the landlord told them made them shiver.

Old Ned could never have been drinking with them as he was one of the men lost at sea all those years ago.

Meanwhile outside two figures glided gracefully over the water, swirling backwards and forwards, hand in hand, through the mist: not so sad now, as they had each other and they are both at rest.

A Black Night
by Liz Penn

The furniture removal man placed the last small chair on the dining room floor and gave an inward sigh of relief. Olive thanked him for all of his hard work and after paying him handsomely said her goodbyes.

Hands on her hips she looked around her, well she had done it now and she was here, this old house is where she and Jim would be spending the rest of their lives together. Thinking of Jim, she wondered where he was and, as if in answer to her thoughts, a voice came down the stairs calling her to come up quickly. Olive slowly mounted the stairs into the bathroom and there he stood, holding a sink plunger...and gazing at an overflowing wash basin.

Well this is a good start thought Olive, she looked at her husband of three months only. Admittedly he had been her lodger for the previous five years, but being married to him was proving what a completely different person he was. Eighty-one-year-old Jim had asked her to marry him and, at the age of seventy-eight herself, she had thought, 'Why not?'

She was fond of the old fella, but she knew he would never take the place of her Charlie, who had been dead a long time. After all, she had been feeling quite lonely. At the registry office wedding, as they tied the knot, they were accompanied by her son Jack, and Jim's daughter Doreen. This was followed by a lovely meal at the Toby Inn, with a glass of Champagne each when they all arrived home, later on.

Four weeks went by and the couple decided that they didn't want to live in their small two-bedroom flat: they needed more space, so they decided to splash their savings on something better, larger, and more grand.

Jim had found the house. It had been empty for many years, the price suited them, and as Jim said to Olive it had lots of potential, and he was also a dab hand at repair jobs. Lucky for them their flat was sold very quickly, a young couple living together were desperate for somewhere to live: it met their budget, and after solicitor appointments and fees paid the couple were ready to move in. This suited Olive and Jim admirably because now the old house was empty they wanted to move as soon as possible. However, as Olive watched Jim trying desperately to un-bung the bathroom wash basin, she began to wonder if this had been such a good idea after all.

Jim decided to leave the basin for a little while, and help to move a few boxes and other items. It was now getting towards evening and Olive had bought some shop sandwiches for them. She decided to make a cup of tea first and – drat it – the kettle would not boil. Jim decided the plug needed a new fuse and, after he put one in, the kettle still wouldn't boil. Olive wondered if he had put the fuse in the right way but kept her thoughts to herself until they had tried the light switches and found that they had no lighting either. With no candles or matches, and just where the torch was was anyone's guess. What a muddle everything seemed to be; it really was turning into a memorable day.

The weary couple managed to sit down on the boxes which had been placed in the kitchen for them to unpack. Olive handed over the sandwiches and Jim managed to find two mugs. He filled them with water so they did have a drink too, when suddenly they heard it: a ghostly whine and whooo, whoooooo, it went, whooooooooo again. Olive screamed, remembering that it was October 31st and Halloween, and that there was a large graveyard at the back of this house. Whooooooo, Whoooooo, Whoooooo: it was all quite alarming. Then she heard something else: loud snores coming from her beloved new husband – he was sound asleep.

After a long dark night, dawn started to break; it was getting lighter, and then the sun streamed through the dusty windows. Jim and Olive jumped up as they heard loud knocking on the front door. She crept cautiously towards it, and carefully opened it, to see a pretty middle-aged lady standing there, who introduced herself as Mary Jones, their neighbour. She explained that she would have come last night, but for the lengthy power cut they had had, lasting for a good few hours. She handed Olive a bunch of Pink carnations which Olive thanked her for, along with her kind thoughts, and as she was turning away the woman stepped back and asked if they had heard him last night, 'up to his old tricks, that old barn owl who sits on the post at the bottom of the garden, and if there are no lights on he sits and hoots the night away.'

Olive realised that Jim had gone back upstairs to the bathroom by now, so she made a mental note to add to the list of 'jobs to do' after he had un-bunged that sink. There was a post now, at the bottom of the garden, to be removed as soon as possible.

The Adopted Daughter
by Phyl Furniss

Paula and Jon had adopted Jessica when she was only a few weeks old. Paula was unable to have children.

Now Jessica was a pretty girl of twenty one years. She had obtained her A levels, went to college and was now working as a private secretary, a job she enjoyed. Her boss was a middle aged man with a wife and growing family, a man who understood young people. Jessica often shared her problems with him, the main one being, 'who were her real parents?' All her childhood they had fobbed her off if the subject was mentioned. Why couldn't her adopted parents tell her? Jessica so desperately wanted to know and was determined now to discover who they were. But where to start?

Her boss told Jessica she must consult her adopted parents first; it could be very hurtful to go behind their backs, he warned. So she decided now was the time to tackle them on the subject. She chose to broach the subject when they settled in the lounge after their evening meal. Tonight would be ideal she thought; they were both free of any engagements and she wasn't seeing Adam, her boyfriend, till later.

As soon as the meal ended and Paula and Jon went through to the lounge to read their newspapers, Jessica 'took the bull by the horns. 'Mum, Dad, I need to talk to you both.'

'Must it be now?' asked Jon.

'Well yes, there's something I need to know.'

'Your father likes to relax with his paper now. You know that Jessica, surely it can wait till later?

'No, Mum, it can't. I've waited too long already and I'm not waiting any longer.'

Her father looked at her over the top of his newspaper. 'What is so important that it can't wait, Jess?'

She hesitated, then spoke. 'I'm talking about my natural parents. I want to know who they were and why they didn't want me.' There, she'd said it. The words burst out of her mouth; in a way she was angry, frustrated. No way was she going to let them put her off any more.

Jon put down his newspaper, took off his glasses and looked straight at his wife. 'Paula,' he said. 'I think Jessica has a right to know. We don't want her to go behind our backs or anything. Besides it would be difficult for her, she wouldn't know where to start.'

Paula's eyes glistened. 'Aren't we good enough for her? She has a lovely home, we've given her a good education... we've always done our best for her...' Paula began to cry.

Jessica ran over to her mother. 'Mummy, darling, please don't cry. I love you and Daddy to bits and I always will. I'm just curious to know... what they were like. Why they had me and then gave me away.' She put her arms around Paula's shoulders and kissed her.

'I've always dreaded this moment, when you would really want to know about them. I suppose.' She wiped her eyes. 'Now is as good a time as any to tell you the truth.' She cried a little more and Jessica hugged her.

Jon said, 'Sit down Jess, I'll tell you...' He waited until his wife and child were settled together on the sofa and Paula had dried her eyes. He paced up and down, stared out of the window, turned and walked towards them, then sat down again in his chair and faced them.

'Your mother, Jessica, was a career woman and your father, a highly respected business man. He was married with a wife and two children. Neither he nor your mother wanted a scandal, which, if it got out that you were on the way, would have damaged his career: his marriage, in all probability, would have ended in divorce, thus hurting his wife and children, and your mother's career as a top model would have been over. The shame of an illegitimate baby twenty-odd years ago was enormous.

I knew them both well,' he continued. 'And they asked if I would adopt their baby. Your mother moved to the country, where no-one knew her, to have you, but soon she would want to return to her career. After a lot of thought and discussion, Paula and I decided to adopt you. Later, your parents went their own ways: your father and his family moved abroad and we lost touch with them. Sadly, your mother never really got over your birth. She pined for you, took to drink and died quite young. We vowed to keep this from you though we knew, one day, we would have to tell you the truth, to share it with you. We both love you,' he smiled. 'We think of you as OUR child.'

Jessica was silent. She squeezed Paula's hand, stood up and walked over to Jon. He took her hand and held it to his lips. He whispered, 'You are our daughter, we'll always be here for you my darling. Please understand; we really wanted you. So did your mother: she'd made a mistake and she paid dearly for it.'

Jessica leaned over to him and kissed Jon's cheek. 'Thank you Dad, thank you both.' She paused. 'I need time to think about this, to take it all in.' She wiped tears from her eyes and left the room. Alone in her bedroom, she pondered over these revelations. She had a good life; member of the ladies' tennis club, went barn dancing with Adam and lots of other social evenings with him. She had known Adam since their schooldays, and they were happy together. Her diary was full of future dates, future plans. She enjoyed her job, although it would soon be time to move on to something else. Now she knew about her parents, she felt happier, but still wanted to know more. It would be easier now to talk about it to Mummy and Daddy.

She tidied herself and prepared to meet Adam, and tell him what she had learned tonight. He would understand, she knew, and would let her ramble on. She was confident he would listen, and give her the support she needed. Paula and Jon had given her all their love, kindness and understanding and she was grateful, They had guided her through childhood, the teen years, given her an excellent education and help to find the job she was now in. She loved them both but still wondered what her life would have been like with her birth parents. 'One day,' she thought, 'I would like to meet my real father: maybe he could tell me if I was like her, my mother.' Perhaps Jon and Paula knew and would tell her: best to leave it, for now, before she asked them more. Briefly, she wondered about half brothers and sisters. Maybe she might even find them on the internet? For now she was satisfied...

A House in the Outback
by Rosemarie David

She stood alone amidst the dust, scrubland and broken fences. Her empty, cracked windows gazed at me forlornly while her corrugated-iron roof-sheets were rusted, loose, and sliding off in places. Some of the brick was crumbling from her walls and beside her the windmill stood still. The rusty empty water tank leaned at a dangerous angle a few feet away.

A heat haze shimmered all around me as I stepped up onto the porch and in through the open doorway. The door had fallen in and lay along the floor of the front room. The smell that lingered was one of despair and loneliness. As I wandered from room to room, taking in the crumbling ruin, my heart was heavy and tears stung my eyes.

I remembered her as she was in my youth: a warm haven that kept me safe from the outside world. The wood stove belching out heat with a pot of mutton stew bubbling on her solid plate. Mother humming as she laid the table.

Dad, having washed his hands, was always ready for his supper. He worked hard and his arms were wiry and strong. Our furnishings were simple, often hand-made but worth more to us than the fancy goods in the city shops.

Yes, our house in the outback could tell many tales of laughter and tears. I was humbled by my last visit to see her before the sale went through. No doubt the new owner would demolish her and build a spacious eco-friendly dwelling. My parents were buried on this land and I had requested that my ashes be scattered near their graves when my time came.

As I turned and walked slowly to my car I was sure I heard a whisper. I looked back as the sun touched a window pane. The old house seemed to wink at me as the echo lingered, 'Goodbye Suzy.'

The Vision
by Sue Whiting

I saw her vision in the window,
She seemed to stand and stare.
I couldn't quite believe it,
Because I knew she wasn't there.

We stared hard at each other,
I felt my blood run cold.
She wasn't very young.
I could tell she looked quite old.

We knew the house was empty,
But the camera never lies:
We knew she held a story,
The one where she just dies.

Will we ever know her secret?
Or is it beyond the grave
That her story lies embedded,
For future years to save?

That's Life
by Louise McClean

From the depths of deep sleep Anna heard the baby cry. She lay there semi-conscious and prayed he would settle again, but no such luck. Her husband Andy appeared to be either deaf or dead so she shuffled next door, with semi-closed eyes, picked up Tom from his cot and put him into the bed between herself and Andy, thus ensuring that none of them would get a decent night's sleep. She really must be more firm; this was ridiculous because Tom was nearly a year now.

The alarm clock blared in Anna's ear and she slapped it off and snuggled down for another few minutes sleep. Fifteen minutes later she came to, sat bolt upright and pulled the bedclothes off her husband – they were late, again. The baby slept on blissfully while Andy and she sprang into action. She grabbed her dressing gown, shouted to the children to get up, and rushed downstairs.

Feverishly she looked for bread to make the packed lunches but the loaf appeared to be finished so it would have to be school dinners again. Had she any money, she wondered? Probably not.

Loud angry protests from above told her that (a) Andy couldn't find an ironed shirt, (b) son Joe couldn't find his PE kit, and (c) daughter Eve had discovered another spot on her face. From the laundry basket she retrieved a shirt for Andy that was almost clean, remembered that the PE kit (unwashed) was in the car boot, and promised to get Eve some magic cream from Boots when she went shopping later. In the absence of toast (no bread) she persuaded everyone to have cereal. This produced more problems, as no-one wanted any of the four brands available. It was with a great sigh of relief that she shoved father and children out of the door towards the car and ran upstairs to retrieve the now yelling Tom.

Baby fed and dirty dishes swooshing around in the dishwasher, Anna sat down with a cup of coffee and planned her day. Today she would clean the whole house, do some washing, and get down to some serious ironing – Andy had not been a happy bunny this morning. Then she would bake some cakes, go to the shops, and later prepare a special meal, to make amends for the disastrous start to the day. She put Tom down for his lap and had just got out the Hoover when the doorbell rang.

On the doorstep her friend Debbie stood, with tears pouring down her cheeks. Anna brought her into the kitchen, hugged her, and gave her a coffee before sitting down to hear the whole story. Debbie was convinced her husband was having an affair with his secretary. She was both heartbroken and furious, was going to leave him and the children, go straight to the office to trash his car, and let the whole office know what a lying rat-bag he was.

By the time Anna had calmed Debbie down, and convinced her she was imagining things, it was well past lunchtime and Anna had done none of the things she had planned. The house was still a tip, the pile of ironing remained untouched, and as she hadn't been to the shops there would be no exciting meal this evening: it looked like eggs and chips again. Oh dear!

Debbie finally left just as the children arrived back from school. They had both had dreadful days. Eve had fallen out with her best friend, because she had laughed at her spot – oh hell, no cream, remembered Anna. Joe hadn't been able to play rugby, because there was only one boot in his bag and it seemed that was all Anna's fault. She attempted to placate them as she cleared a place at the table so, hopefully, their homework could begin. She was worried about the baby, who seemed to have earache and was yelling nonstop, and refusing to be let down. So, with child anchored on hip, she began to prepare the gourmet egg-and-chips meal.

When Andy arrived home he looked about ninety, and it appeared his day had also been disastrous – a valuable contract had been lost and he had had to chair a meeting wearing a grubby shirt: her fault again, naturally.

The evening meal was received by all in sullen silence, and it was a great relief when 9:30 came and the children went to bed. Anna quickly ironed two shirts and a blouse.

Slumping into a chair in front of the TV, she prepared to spend some 'quality time' with Andy. In the middle of telling him of Debbie's visit, she noticed he was fast asleep and snoring softly; so much for having discussions with your partner.

Eve appeared downstairs again, saying she had cookery first thing in the morning and needed to have macaroni, cheese, flour, margarine, and milk. Now where, Anna thought, was she supposed to find all that before morning, and why was she not told before the shops closed? There was a tin of macaroni cheese in the cupboard: maybe that would do instead.

Around eleven o'clock she made a cup of coffee for the still-groggy Andy and they went up to bed. Anna had a shower and was just drifting off to sleep when she suddenly remembered she hadn't taken any bread out of the freezer, so down she went to the bitterly-cold garage to do this.

'At last,' she sighed as she settled into bed and was just snuggled nicely into Andy's back when, to her despair, she heard a familiar wail coming from the baby's room. 'Oh no, not again,' said poor, long-suffering Anna as she threw back the covers once more.

No Goodbye
by Olga Tramontin

I'll leave you now, my sweet, among these trees where once we walked hand in hand as so in love. Your ashes I have covered with a blanket of leaves, damp and heavy they are with tears of saddest winter and my own. Now I return to a lonely cottage that once we shared for all those years. The fire is ready for me to light. See you very soon, my love.

Every Day is a New Beginning
by Carol Campbell

A fresh start
With new growth
Where you see something new
Something a little different
We all learn
It maybe a simple task
But it builds in our book of knowledge
Giving us a new out look
Another chance
New opportunities
Nothing happens without a reason
It happens to enable us to grow
Not just in stature
But also in strength
It also teaches us to understand
So we can look in anothers eyes
And feel with empathy
As we know how to walk forward

And we can hold out a hand
To help someone
To enable them to find direction
To move forward.

A Wise Woman
by Rosemarie David

A small fire burned low in the tepee and the old woman drew the pale blue blanket closer around herself. Her hair hung like a thick silver rope down her back and her face was weary. With faded brown eyes she looked into the tearstained face of her granddaughter.

'It is my time to return to the ancestors' child: do not weep.' Gently she placed her hand on the child's chest above her heart. 'You shall cradle me here within you: you shall feel my touch in the breeze and hear my laughter in the gurgling river and while you live I shall not be gone from you.'

Laughing Dove looked at the beloved face of her grandmother and asked 'But why do you need to go, Grandmother?'

'All must return to Mother Earth child, and when your time comes you will understand: you are young and have many paths to travel, but my moccasins are worn and my bones tired. One day you will feel the strong arms of your husband around you and cradle your babe in your own.'

Outside the tepee another woman stood and wept silently as she listened to her mother say goodbye to her granddaughter. 'Come child' the old woman continued. 'It is late and the stars multiply in the sky, it is time for you to sleep.' The little girl stood up and gave her grandmother a fierce hug and a wet kiss before crawling beneath the pile of buffalo-skins and closing her eyes. Only then did the tears pour down the old woman's wrinkled face.

A few days later the child and her mother stood at the funeral pyre of the woman known as Summer Rain with the rest of the tribe. The child's face suddenly lit up as a faint breeze touched her cheek and she exclaimed loudly, 'I feel you, Grandmother.' Gazing one last time at the faces of her daughter and granddaughter the old woman gently took her hand from the child's face and turning away she walked toward the curls of smoke that drifted upwards into the sky.

April Love
by Phyl Furniss

Softly, softly the April breeze caresses her soft brown hair
As she stands beneath the old oak tree.
How she wishes with all her heart that he, too, was there.

She listens to the gentle rain as it splatters on the leaves.
Her heart is so full of love for the one she wants to please.
So why this look of sadness as she stands beneath the tree?

Does she have a secret she doesn't want to share?
Perhaps he's been away so long, she thinks he doesn't care?
Maybe it's the thought of when they're wed, she no longer will be free?

If only he could see her as she stands beneath the tree,
The warmth and living beauty of a goddess young and free.
Come back to her, take her in your arms, your love for her proclaim
Because you love her dearly, that love will never change.

The Verdict
by Maureen Thomas

They were waiting for the jury to come to a decision. The small room they were waiting in was cramped and windowless which made them feel like prisoners themselves. The court attendant kept coming in to see if they were ok, but they wouldn't be until that animal was put away and for a very long time.

Angela, who was now 11 years old, and her mother, Stephanie, had been through hell and back and although it had only taken ten months to get here, it had seemed like ten years.
Stephanie's marriage to Angela's father was over and she now lived with her new partner Eddy. Angela, who was only six at the time of the break up, had to remain (for various reasons) with her father and three older brothers, plus one younger brother, in the marital home, and they visited on a regular basis. All very amicable, or so Stephanie thought. Five years had passed. The clock in the room ticked so slowly.

Stephanie allowed her mind to wander back to the night it all started. She was getting ready for a night out with Eddy when the telephone rang. 'Oh bother,' she said to herself. She went into the hall and picked up the receiver. She didn't realise who it was at first as the voice was very faint and then she couldn't believe her own ears.

It was Angela and she was pleading to come to her house, she had got her small brother with her at the phone box down their road and she was sobbing and pleading to come and live with her and said she couldn't take any more. 'Any more what?' Stephanie asked.

It was then, in between sobs, Angela said her father had been doing things with her, and she had finally had enough.

Stephanie went into over drive when she realised what had been happening. Her heart thudding faster and faster she just about managed to tell her daughter to wait for a taxi that would bring her and her brother to safety.

She paced anxiously backwards and forwards until that taxi arrived at their front door and when her two children finally emerged, she very quickly ushered them into the living room while Eddy paid the taxi man. They came as they were, no extra clothes, nothing, just the enormous burden of what had been happening.

She looked awful, so pale and gaunt and her eyes were red rimmed from all the crying: her little brother didn't really know what was going to happen. He thought it was an adventure travelling with his sister in a taxi (he was only seven, bless him).

After a warm drink and something to eat, Eddy took Angela's brother for a walk with the dog, and Stephanie listened to her daughter's sad story; of how her ex-husband started to touch her in a way that she knew was wrong, saying that if she told anyone she would not be able to visit her mum again.

This had apparently been going on for quite some time. .It was very strange, that Stephanie had thought for a while that something was odd when her daughter kept asking to stay with her and saying that she didn't want to go home. She thought it was just because they had such a good time together on their visits and that her ex-husband was rather strict with them all. She had supposed he had to be in a way.

After calling the police, which was the only thing she could do, another round of questions took place. It was quite a long evening. When the police finally left, they warned Stephanie not to talk to anyone about this. 'As if', Stephanie thought. It was hardest when knew she had to ring her ex-husband to say that the two of them were staying for a while as it was the school holidays and she needed some of their clothes. She told him to send them round by taxi. She couldn't even say anything to him about the real reason they were staying, which was the hardest

116

thing. Deep down she wanted to put a hammer to his head for what he had put his only daughter through.

The police took ten whole months to gather all the evidence needed.

Stephanie was abruptly brought back to reality when the court attendant brought them yet another cup of tea and she asked how much longer the jury would be out. As if by magic, a very official man in a long black cloak summoned her to come to the court room because the jury had reached their verdict.

Stephanie and Angela held tightly to each other as they followed the man down the long twisty corridors, his cape flying so wide he was almost gliding.

The big double doors were opened for them and they were directed to the public gallery. The jury was ready to give their verdict. Stephanie's heart was beating so loudly she thought everyone in the court room must have heard it.

They stood when the judge came in and then they were allowed to sit down, all except the accused who stood in the dock like he hadn't got a care in the world. The judge asked the representative of the jury if they had reached a decision and was it unanimous?

'Yes,' said the man. 'We have.'

Stephanie held her daughter tightly; both were shaking with nerves.

'What is your verdict?' asked the judge.

'Guilty,' the man said.

The accused went to prison for ten years.

As they walked out of the court room Stephanie and Angela stopped and hugged and cried with relief. Then Angela said, 'Thank you Mum for believing in me.'

SOS
by Phyl Furniss

Not another conked out car!
It really is too bad
Just filled up with petrol, hasn't got me far,
Said I'd meet a mate, he's waiting at the bar.
Rang him on my mobile, he really is a star
Coming out to fetch, he is a real good lad
Better pay his petrol, though he's not come far
On second thoughts I'll buy the drinks
Or else he'll think I'm mad...

Gypsy of the Past
by Carol Campbell

An old lady wearing clothes from a bygone day sat across an open room. 'My child I need to speak to you,' she softly spoke in a whispered voice, her frail fading fingers gently holding a cup of the finest bone china.

Just as her tea evaporated into her thirst with every breath, the transparent bone revealed no shadow – almost as if there was an empty space.

Her trembling fingers reached out, 'Let me hold your hand, my precious child. I'll read your palm for a silver crown.'

My eyes met hers in disbelief.

She must have read my mind as I watched her lips turn into a gentle smile. In her hushed voice she whispered, 'You have travelled far on this twisted road and carried much weighted baggage. You've lost and won many a battle, you've been a hero. But you've also been saved.'

As she rambled on, in what seemed like broken English, she spoke of memories that raised some smiles, but some also persuaded gentle tears.

Her eyes spoke of love that needed to be sent by the shadows of the past.

The feeling was warm and harmonious as I gently closed my eyes to wrap myself in the not so distant memories. I opened them in disbelief.

As I sat alone in the hushed silence, the frail old lady had escaped my view. All that remained was the musty smell, an aroma of the past, since evaporated.

Molly's Special Christmas Tree
by Rosemarie David

It was a bitterly cold Christmas morning and Molly made her way carefully along the dark passage and into the sitting room which was filled with the scent of pine. Walking over to the tree she buried her face in the sweet smelling spiky branches and smiled to herself. Her Daddy had promised her a special tree this year and she knew that he would keep his word. Gently her fingers moved over the smooth glass ornaments, candy canes, fluffy tinsel and gingerbread cookies tied with ribbons.

Daniel entered the room and softly walked towards his daughter who on hearing him turned and holding out her arms asked quietly 'Please let me see the Angel on top Daddy'. Her six year old voice was squeaky with excitement. Two strong arms lifted her up onto his shoulders and leaning forward she ran her fingers over the silk skirt and gossamer wings of the golden haired Angel. 'Can Mommy see her too Daddy?' she asked and as Daniel lowered her to the floor he answered 'Yes darling, Mommy can see all of us because she lives with the angels now.'

Molly threw her little arms around his legs and smiling up at him she said 'Oh Daddy it is the most beautiful Christmas tree I have ever seen'. Daniel placed his hand softly on her tumbled curls and trying to hold back the sob that rose to his throat he bent down to hug her. A tear slid slowly down his cheek because the tragic car accident that had taken his beloved wife and Molly's Mother a year ago had also robbed his precious daughter of her sight.

The Problem with Roman Soldiers
by Olga Tramontin

The idea was... to move the heavy plinth and its even heavier Roman head from one end of the garden to the other. 'Roll it on logs' someone suggested. Fine except, because their house was centrally heated, there was no fireplace and therefore no logs needed.

'Cut down some branches and use them instead,' said someone else. All very well in theory, but when she examined her trees she doubted whether an acer, an apple tree, two bamboos, a waving Japanese willow or the wild, flowering cherry that had invaded their garden three years ago had enough straight branches between them to facilitate a rolling-log mode of transport.

'I wonder if the Druids had this much trouble, when they brought in the monoliths to make Stonehenge,' she wondered. 'And all I want to do is move a flaming statue from one end of the garden to the other: shouldn't need rocket science.'

She'd seen films of the Egyptians (Hollywood style admittedly) moving amazingly heavy stones to build the pyramids, and that took place thousands of years ago before the wheel was invented.

'How about,' began her husband, who then paused, shook his head and said, 'no that wouldn't work.'

'What wouldn't work?' she asked.

'It doesn't matter.'

They must be the most frustrating words anyone has to listen to.

'What doesn't matter?'

'I've just told you, it wouldn't work.'

She gave up in disgust and made herself a cup of tea, took it out to the garden and stared at the unseeing eyes of the Roman centurion. Perhaps I should take up weightlifting she thought. Or make him do it: him being her 'it doesn't matter' husband.

'Hello, Mrs T.' It was her next door neighbour's little boy greeting her over the garden fence.

'Hello Sam. How are you?'

'I'm fine Mrs T. You alright?'

'Yes thank you Sam,' she lied.

She sipped her tea and watched the boy play. He had slung a piece of rope over a lower branch of the apple tree in his garden, and was heave-ho-ing one of his metal trucks off the ground and swinging it towards his toy wheelbarrow.

She watched fascinated as he pulled on one end of the rope and saw the truck gradually reaching the height of his empty wheelbarrow. As soon as he had swung it in place, he let go the rope and his truck gave a clunk as it landed inside. He then wheeled it towards the house where he tipped it out onto his sandpit.

She looked again at Cicero (Cicero was what she called the Roman soldier). Right, young man. You'll be moving, as soon as I can find a rope and put the wheelbarrow in place.

'Lawrence,' she yelled out. She knew her husband would come soonest if she called him by his full name, not Laurie or Lol.

'What's up?'

'Nothing,' she smiled at him. 'I've solved the problem of moving Cicero.'

'Oh yeah?'

'Pulley,' she said.

'Pulley?' he repeated.

Gently she explained the plan. Thankfully, at the end of her explanation, he nodded. 'Yes,' he said. 'I can see that working, as long as the apple tree can take his weight.'

An hour later, after much heaving and ho-ing, Cicero stood proudly (can a head and shoulders stand?) Ok, correction: Cicero rested proudly on his newly-positioned plinth at the other end of the garden. 'He looks quite noble', she thought, under the shade of the purple maple leaves. And the rose growing next to him really suited him: took away some of the greyness of the stone he was made of. Thanks Sam, she thought. Out of the mouth and minds of babes...

Problems and Progress
by Carol Campbell

Think before you speak,
Words can cause a lot of damage,
Even when you have forgotten,
The recipient will remember,

The pain will still be etched somewhere,
Under the surface.
When you walk past a stranger,
Smile, don't frown.
They may not look like they're from your street,
But what of it?
They could have a very deep meaningful knowledge,
That could help you along your road
To progress, and learn just that little bit more.

To progress, you learn that little more from some of the poorest
And loneliest people.
This could solve a lot of the world's problems,
With their voices having been heard.

Another Life
by Liz Penn

'Does she always sit hunched up in that corner, alone and silent?' The new carer was talking about Ada, the very elderly lady sitting in the corner of the large dining room. She didn't seem to want to socialize with anyone , just sat in her corner with a little smile playing about her lips from time to time.

Mrs Wood, the supervisor of St Catherine's, answered by saying that Ada made a point of going out at least three times a week. She went on her own down the road to the derelict church of St Bartholomew's. 'We think she sits for many hours reminiscing about the old days. We don't bother her because she seems to enjoy what she does.'
The young carer shrugged her shoulder's saying, 'she sounds a bit silly to me.' and carried on with her duties.

Ada wasn't silly and she wasn't deaf either. She overheard the conversation and then, with a wry smile, glanced at the clock on the wall. Five minutes later, with her walking stick in hand, Ada was stepping out through the door of St Catherine's on her journey to St Bartholomew's. She walked slowly, so it took her a good half hour to get there, and surprisingly her steps got lighter as she walked up the path, towards the entranceway of the derelict church building.

The voices were loud and demanding, 'More nurses are needed here, we have wounded soldiers arriving shortly. The men will have had a long journey, from a hospital train to a ship and then by ambulance, to our hospital here .today. Where is Ada? She is needed in surgery, there will be many limbs lost today.'

'I am here now.' And there she was: Ada, a beautiful nurse dressed ready in her grey uniform and white apron with the red cross emblazoned on the front.

Little time for talking, the ambulances were coming in now packed full of bloodied, wounded men. Ada, along with the other nurses and the volunteer VADs, never stopped. She assisted the surgeon with his grisly tasks and comforted the young men: some were crying out for their Mother, others lay just shocked and frightened. She organized clean bed linen for those men already attended to, and read stories to others; she comforted and even joked with a few of them, and promised to write letters to folk at home when asked to do so.

In the early hours, with many of the helpers now resting, Ada walked slowly towards the church attached to the hospital. Just before entering, she turned and saw as always the surgeon looking. She waved her hand and he gave her a goodbye salute, and a nod of thanks and appreciation.

The new carer was looking through the window waiting for Ada to come for her hot milk which was served at supper time. She saw her meandering along the road, walking very slowly. Silly old fool she thought, fancy sitting in that place alone all day, especially when you can join in here with the other residents to play an exciting game of Bingo.

Hide and Sleep
by Ruth Broster

I am the tree that will not weep
I close my eyes and fall asleep
Refusing to let one cut me down
I hide my body in foliage brown

When winter falls with Snow White flakes
I will not be seen till spring awakes
My intertwining branches will be strong once more
My foliage leaves green galore
And when Summer arrives, I am at my best
You will not cut me down
For I have passed the test.

Džien Dobry, Dzieci
by Louise McClean

The day I went to Poland to teach, twenty years ago, was for me a mixture of excitement and near terror, because it was a step into the unknown. Six months previously I had read an article, in a teachers' magazine, appealing for fit retired teachers to do voluntary English teaching in Polish schools for a period of six months or a year.

The idea appealed to me and I applied to the headquarters of Teachers for Poland in Hereford. I had an interview, was accepted, and a few months later was told that I would be going in late August, to join the staff of a high-school in Ostroleka which is a small town in the northwest of Poland, quite near to the Belarus border.

There was a weekend in Hereford where I met other volunteers. We learned what was expected of us and had a brief course in the language – this latter, a complete waste of time in my case.

Six months ago it had all seemed such a good idea, so exciting and challenging. But now, as I stood at Manchester Airport waiting for the plane to Warsaw, I wasn't so sure.

Was I insane? Here I was, going to another country where I knew no-one, didn't speak the language, and facing a notoriously sever winter. To top it all, I was to teach sixth-from children when all of my teaching experience was with much younger pupils.

I said a tearful goodbye to my husband and family and joined Doris, who was another brave or insane teacher – from Liverpool, in the departure hall. We were going to entirely different areas of Poland: she to the south and me to the north, but we promised to get together when we could (and we did).

We were met at Warsaw Airport by two staff members from our host school. In my case it was the headmaster and the teacher of English, Richard and Beata, and they were both lovely. Richard spoke no English but Beata's was excellent. They were so very welcoming that I began to relax at once. My new friend Doris and I said our farewells and set off on our adventures.

It all turned out very well: I had a wonderful time in Poland and enjoyed every minute. The Polish people I met were so kind to me and so generous, though they had so little. I travelled all over the country at the weekends, from Gadansk in the north to Cracow in the south, in the filthy old buses and trains, staying in youth hostels and I learned so much.

My husband came out and joined me for Christmas, which we spent in Cracow with Doris and some other teachers. It was fantastic: the Poles hadn't much money but they certainly knew how to have a good time.

So, as it turned out, I had no need to worry about going to Poland at all. I soon made friends, I survived the bitter winter, the children were a joy to teach, and it wasn't necessary to speak much Polish as a smile will get you anything you need – in any country.

This was one of the best experiences of my life and I will always be grateful for the opportunity.

Tempus Fugit
by Carol Campbell

Time doesn't stand still

We need to make the most of what time we have

Every moment we have is precious

And every moment is worthwhile

Life is like the ebb of the sea

Some days it can be calm

And other days it can be stormy

But remember each day is a lesson

To give us strength and motivation

To tackle the next obstacle

That way those obstacles won't seem so difficult

After the storm the calm will arrive

And no matter how hard it's been

You will be able to look back

And see how far you have travelled and how successful you have become

Because you believed that that calm would reappear

Along with that sunshine from behind the clouds,

So make the most of time

Use it wisely

And as positively as you possibly can.

No one is ever a lost cause

And no one will remain lost forever

Sometimes all it takes is a warm smile

A friendly hello

And a hand held out to help those lost

Find a direction

This is like turning a light on in the darkest place

To show some one there is light at the end of the tunnel

There is a way
And no one needs to remain lost
As there is people waiting for those
So they can be found
and given a little direction
For all the right reasons xx

In life we have to remember
We all move at different paces
Some of us feel we need to run
Some people rather plod by at a snail's pace
We all have different likes
And dislikes
It doesn't make anyone right
Or anyone wrong
Its individual
As we all are
And it is our right
And everyone else's right
To be just that
Individual.

Letters
by Sue Whiting

Dearest Irene,

What a joy it was to see you at the annual square knitting gathering. I was so pleased that you made the effort to come, I know you haven't felt yourself of late. Did you tell your doctor about the problems you were having, or were you too embarrassed to? I am so glad I've got a lady doctor because, with my problems, I feel it is a necessity.

Have I told you about my problem down below? Yes I must have done. Well, to cut a long story short. I went to my doctor and she put my mind at rest...and after all that worry.

Anyway, are you going to make it over to tea on the 8th of this month? It would be so lovely to see you again, and it gives me the excuse to get my best bone china out. And I can make us a nice Victoria sponge. What do you think?

I had that gardener fellow over to do my borders last week. You should see them now, they look a picture. But I think he charges too much. And would you believe this – I think he has an eye for ,e. I know I'm no spring chicken, but I can still pull them, I can tell you. But I know he's married and me, being a good Christian woman and all that, well I mustn't give him a second chance. I don't want to encourage him or anything, do I?

Guess where I went last Wednesday? I went swimming! Remember I was telling you about doing more exercise, well I decided swimming was the way. I quite enjoyed it in the end, and will definitely go again. I met a lady who was 84, who goes swimming every week. That's when she's not out walking or going to keep fit classes. Well I ask you, she put me to shame.

I had a senior moment last week. My son was having a look at my car when the alarm went off. I told him I didn't even know it had an alarm. He quickly took a good look over it, tried to turn everything off. He then suggested I call the RAC. He had another quick look inside and found I'd pulled my personal alarm on the key ring by mistake. I did feel silly, especially as I was wondering why the alarm was louder in the car than outside.

Anyway, Irene, I'd best finish now and go and get this posted. I do hope you're feeling better and look forward to seeing you on the 8th,

Best wishes, Vera.

Dearest Vera

It was so lovely to hear from you this morning. I sat with my usual tipple, with Cuddles on my lap, and read your letter in comfort.

Fancy you swimming! You are brave Vera. I certainly wouldn't have the courage to do it at our age. Gosh, that 84 year old woman must be so fit. As I told you before, I don't do exercise. Cuddles is quite happy walking round the garden, otherwise he goes in the car with me. I suppose the most exercise I get is walking to the car.

I think you're very brave swimming. Did you have to buy a much bigger costume like you said you might have to? Or were you ok in your old one? I hope you don't mind me saying this, but I noticed with the weight you've put on recently, your clothes seem to be a bit on the restricted side.

I hope to make it over on the 8th. It would be lovely to see you again. It was so good to see you at the annual square knitting ceremony. It was a bit of a do wasn't it? I thought Lady Goff looked unsightly in that pink mini thing. You'd think a lady of her status and senior years would be more sensibly dressed wouldn't you?

And Sir Geoffrey with his roving eyes and hands. He gets worse each year. Twice I had to remove his hand from...what you might call embarrassing positions. Talking of embarrassing positions – fancy your gardener giving you the eye. Well, I'll tell you my dear, he could give me the eye any time. He's a hunk. Take your chances with him, live dangerously!

Well my dear, I'd better get on. I've got my WI meeting in an hour, so best get ready and put my face on. Do hope this finds you well, and I'll look forward to the 8th.

Fondest regards, Irene

The Old Man
by Phyl Furniss

An old man was going in search of a home
For many a year he had been all alone.
A garden of flowers, a babbling brook
Sun, moon and clouds would enhance a nook.
Clasping fond memories of days long ago
His dreams fulfilled? Only he would know.

As he lumbered along, cold wind on his face
A hole in a rock could be such a place
Where a shepherd once cared for his flock of sheep
A place where he could lie down and sleep.
His hand hid his face as he looked around
Admiring wild flowers he saw so profound

Fresh air flowing from over high hills
A warm log fire to keep out cold chills
A babbling brook, sun, moon, and clouds
Yes, he had found his home away from the crowds.

The Village Fete
by Maureen Thomas

It was the day of the annual village fete and the weather looked like it was going to be kind. The sun was shining while a gentle breeze made the brightly coloured bunting dance and bob above the small river that gurgled its way down the main street.

'It's going to be a fine affair,' so the vicar's wife said. The previous year was simply chaos, what with the fight after the cake competition between two of the main rivals. They came each year with their creations and they each thought that they were better than the other. This year it was quite simply a decorated Victoria sponge or fancy fairy cakes: now what could go wrong there?

People were beginning to filter into the large field where the main marquee proudly stood. The local school band had started to play and there was a good atmosphere all around. There was a juggler walking around on stilts, and a stall where children could win a small prize if they knocked a coconut off its stand and, as I strolled around a little more, I noticed a hot dog stall and the smell drifting around was making me hungry.

A tent had been set up for Gypsy Rose Lee, who read your palm for a small donation. There were lots of different stalls, but new this year were the duck race on the river where the local children would put their name on the bottom of the duck and place it in the water and hope that they reached the little bridge at the end of the road. They were so excited as they waited for the race to start: it was almost lunch time and there was still plenty to see.

I made my way past the various stalls to another tent where there was a' biggest vegetable' competition going on. I can honestly say that I have never in all my life seen such big onions! They were the size of footballs.

Also new this year was the pet show and over the tannoy it was announced that this was about to start in the large field at the end of the village, near the river. So over I strolled. There was a great assortment of dogs there ranging from sheep dogs and lurchers to tiny little terriers. It was time for the obedience test: a German Shepherd dog went first and as expected it did everything correctly. A border terrier was next and despite a couple of tiny mistakes he also got through. Now it was the turn of the Jack Russell. His name was Feef. Well, Feef who often lived up to his name didn't do very well I'm afraid, because he saw a football in the middle of the arena, slipped his lead and promptly made a bee line for it. He ran like the wind while in complete control of the ball, dribbling his way to where the duck race was about to start. But before that he had to pass a rather large lady sitting on the grass enjoying a picnic with her friends. She was about to push a hot dog into her large open mouth when, to her and everyone else's surprise, Feef ran up and snatched it right out of her hand and ran off with it dangling out of his mouth. It did not take long for that sausage to disappear though and as soon as he had devoured it, he ran straight towards the main marquee where the cake competition was in progress. OH NO!

No one could catch this four legged thief as he made a bee line for the big table at the top where the cake rivals were standing proudly beside their Victoria sponges. By now, a few more dogs had joined in, and chaos reigned supreme, The two rivals were shocked as the dogs started pulling at the table cloths where their precious cakes were balancing precariously on the edge of the table. They both turned to try to rescue them but they didn't make it. They slipped over themselves , bumped heads and slipped to the ground where their cakes landed beside them, butter cream splashed all over their faces. There they sat with their dresses up to their waists, bloomers on show, slightly concussed and very embarrassed at their predicament...

That was the last fete ever held in the village. Shame really, it was the funniest one that I'd ever been to.

Buzy Bee
by Ruth Broster

When I went to Snowshill one day
Not knowing what I would see,
I had heard about Charles Wade
And how he was a busy bee
Walking along his garden path
With lovely views galore
Flowers blooming everywhere
Many colours I do adore

This charming house in age old stone
Holds history in its name
Once belonging to Henry
The king! you know his name

With Charles loving life
Not letting time fly by
He travelled far with interest
Saw things that caught his eye

Brought items home and laid them out
For everyone to see
Restored the beauty with his own hands
No wonder he was a busy bee.

When I Went Back
by Olga Tramontin

Davey told me years ago, when the swing was new, that it was really a gallows, and two murderers were due to be hung from it. I ran away, 'You're a liar, Davey Banks. I'm telling Mum you lied.' I was crying.

It was painted blue. They don't paint gallows that colour, do they? Dan followed me, confident as always. He didn't care if I believed him or not. Davey didn't care about anything. He was young, we were young. It was summertime.

I never questioned why the swing (or gallows) had been put there. It wasn't there last summer, on our beach of soft white sand that led down to the sea, and back across the dunes to our house. Our house wasn't built of brick like those in the nearby seaside town, but of timber, white boards with pale blue painted windows, two up and two down, and a pitch roof. The window frames, strangely, were the same colour as the swing.

Thick rope dangled from the cross beam and joined the wooden swing seat. Davey said, when I finally finished running, 'you gonna try it?'

'Try what,' I panted, out of breath from running on sand.

'The swing, silly.'

'Dunno,'

'Go on, you sit on it and I'll stand. I'll make it go higher and faster. We can fly.'

'Ok,' I said.

He helped me onto the painted wooden seat. I grasped both pieces of rope, my feet hardly touching the ground. Davey put a foot either side of me and grabbed the rope above me. He bent his knees and began to push backwards and forwards, gaining momentum. Soon we were flying: one minute up in the blue sky, the next flying down towards sandy dunes. I forgot my anger and began to laugh with the joy of it. There were ships out there, fishing trawlers returning to harbour chased by screaming gulls, a scattering of white sail boats, and a small motor boat that sliced its way across the water.

I looked inland and saw Mum outside the house. She shaded her eyes against bright sunlight with one hand and waved to us with the other, beckoning.

'Time for tea,' Davey said, and slowed us down. He jumped off before the swing stopped, landing onto the wild grass that grew amongst the sandy soil. I used my feet as a brake and skipped off.

'Come on,' he said. 'Race you back.'

He won. His legs were longer than mine, stronger. He was built athletically, even at ten: he often talked about being in the Olympics. I was skinny. Spindle he called me.

'Did you see us?' I shouted at Mum as we ran to her. 'We were flying up to the sky.'

She had a serious face, the one she wore if we had bad school reports. She briefly smiled. 'Yes,' she said, and the smile faded again. 'Come inside, I've something to tell you.'

We followed her into the house, our summer home. He was sitting in an armchair by the small fireplace. Mum's boyfriend. Shiny hair slicked back with Brylcream, white open-necked shirt revealing dark curls on his chest; light coloured slacks and sandals.

'Hello you two.' He was grinning and I saw gold in his teeth. He reminded me of a shark, except sharks don't have gold fillings: do they?

Mum went over to him, letting him hold her hand which he squeezed like a sponge.

'Hello Harry,' we said. I looked up at my brother's face. His hooded eyes and set mouth showed no emotion. He put an arm round my shoulder and I snuggled into its warm protection.

Mum said, 'Harry's come to stay for a few weeks.' Her eyes were bright, sunlight freckling her face as the lace curtains blew at the open window.

'How many weeks?' I asked. I suppose it sounded rude, but this was our holiday home that Gran had lent us all summer. Mum said it was because Gran felt guilty about her son going off with that floozy. He was our Dad.

'Don't know,' Mum smiled at him, kind of sweeping Davey and I away with the sand that constantly invaded the house. 'Two, three, maybe more.'

Harry stayed until it was time to return home and us back to school. It had been a different summer. Not one to be enjoyed like the previous two years. Davey said Harry was trying to be Dad.

'We've got a dad,' I said. 'I wish he'd go.'

But that autumn it was us who left. He sent us away to boarding school where we slept six to a room, had grinding lessons every day, and ate our meals there as well. I hated it and cried every night. Davey wasn't even in the adjoining bedroom: he shared a dormitory with five other boys in the Boys' Block. We only met at mealtimes, couldn't even sit together. He grew taller and paler, with red blotches on his face and neck.

'We'll be going home soon,' he told me one teatime. 'Half term.'

He didn't sound enthusiastic.

'Will he be there?' I asked.

'Oh yes... King Harry.'

'So is Mum a queen and me a princess?'

'Don't be daft,' Davey wasn't smiling.

Harry met us at the station, not Mum.

'Got a surprise for you two,' he said. I asked what it was. Davey didn't.

'Wait and see.'

Harry opened the front door and called out, 'we're back.'

I ran through to the kitchen. Mum was there by the sink filling the kettle. I stopped short as I saw her big, swollen tummy.

'Hello darlings.' She sounded different, a stranger, not our Mum. 'You're going to have a baby brother or sister,' and 'Come give us a hug then.'

I ran to her and cuddled her big tummy. She was still our Mum, with her warm caressing hands, smelling of the lemony soap she washed in. Dan walked slowly towards us, standing awkwardly. Mum reached out and tousled his hair.

'My, you've grown son, nearly as tall as me now.'

Harry laughed. It was not a pleasant laugh. 'Not as tall as me though.'

138

The week passed quickly. Mum showed me all the things she had collected for the baby: tiny clothes, a wicker cradle and a smaller, matching basket for baby creams and things. Harry made Davey sweep the leaves from the backyard. Then it was time to go back to school. Strangely I wasn't sorry, neither was Davey. He said to me on the train, 'She must have been pregnant before the summer.'

'How d'you mean?'

'Think about it, a baby takes nine months and it's due in December. She must have been pregnant in April.'

I counted on my fingers. 'Mm,' I said.

When we arrived at the station Davey said, 'I'm not coming into school with you. Might see you later.' And he was gone. I never saw my brother again, only his coffin. Mum lost the baby she was carrying as well.

'It would have been a boy,' she sobbed.

Years later I returned to the summer house. Gran left it to me in her will. I walked down to the beach. The swing frame was still there, but without rope. Davey had hanged himself from it...

Index of Authors

More books from Chadgreen Publishing†

THE CHAMPAGNE WRITERS OF SHROPSHIRE
an anthology by writers from north-east Shropshire

THE STORYTELLER AND OTHER TALES
an anthology by Joan Barlow

A POCKETFUL OF YESTERDAYS
a further anthology by Joan Barlow

KETLEY ESTATE SALE 1894
an historical reference book compiled for (and distributed by)
The Ketley History Group

Coming soon†

READING BETWEEN THE LINES
an anthology by John Cliff and Anna Newman

SEEKING ANNIE
a novel by Olga Tramontin

THE KILLING OF ELLIE SWALES
a novel by Olga Tramontin

† for further information about these titles please email **chadgreenbooks@yahoo.com**